DreamScape II
Gods and Monsters

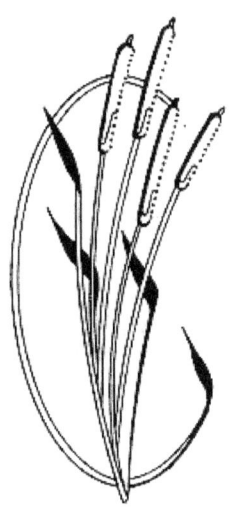

DreamScape II
Gods and Monsters

by
Joshua Jeremiah Hill

Senior Publisher
Steven Lawrence Hill Sr.

ASA Publishing Corporation
ASA Publishing Company

ASA Publishing Corporation
An Accredited Publishing House by the BBB
105 E. Front St., Suite. 101, Monroe, Michigan 48161
www.asapublishingcorporation.com

Copyrights©2016 Joshua Jeremiah Hill, All Rights Reserved
Book title: DreamScape II *Gods and Monsters*
Date Published: 06.29.2016
Edition 1 - *Trade Paperback*
Book ASAPCID: 2380694
ISBN: 978-0-9977790-0-4
Library of Congress Cataloging-in-Publication Data

This book was published in the United States of America.
State of Michigan

"To My Father and My Family"

Table of Contents

DreamScape II *Gods and Monsters*

DreamScape II
Gods and Monsters

by
Joshua Jeremiah Hill

Uneasy Alliance

Uriel was a feisty Angel that was hard to control. Death placed necromantic bonds on her wrists, ankles and wings so she couldn't do anything. The Horsemen, Death and War traveled far enough from the valley to buy them some time. Their horses trotted a few feet further into another valley filled with amazing flowers. "What is this place?" War thought to himself.

"This is far enough," Death hopped off his steed. Uriel was pulled from the saddle and thrown to the ground. War stood behind the Angel while Death stood in front. "What do you want from me now? My life?"

"Careful, before I grant you your wish," Death

said caressing her cheek. Uriel pulled away defiantly. "I don't want your life, I want information from that majestic head of yours. You know where more of these portals are don't you?" Uriel turned away from Death, she didn't want to face the Nephilim. "You're a strong Angel with astounding physical prowess. That strength can only count for so much when the mental will is tested. I will tamper with your mind until your very psyche cracks."

Death held Uriel's head still while potent magic formed around his hands. Uriel wasn't sure if she would be able to withstand such torment on a mystical level. Torment that could seep into every inch of her mind and cause the most excruciating pain ever. Her mind began to numb as the pain intensified as Death tightened his grip. Uriel had to hold on a little longer. The crackling sound of thunder erupted in the sky noting the arrival of a powerful being. It was another Angel, he locked onto the trio's location and zeroed in. He dove at lighting speed like that of a descending comet and pulled up in the nick of time and soared inches above the grass. The Angel came to an abrupt halt right in front of them and landed. "Michael," War said. This Archangel was by far the best ever known. Michael was larger in size than both Death and War combined. There are plenty of stories about this angel. The history between the Four Horsemen and the Archangels is a complicated one. You can say that the recent activity between Death, War, and Uriel complicated it further.

Death didn't have to turn around to know it was Michael. The Pale Rider knew the presence all too well. Michael walked forward and placed a hand on Death's pale flesh. "That's enough Reaper," the Archangel said. The Angel's voice was like that of many flowing rivers. Death wanted to slice the Angel's arm off but the Rider had too much respect for Michael. The magic that formed around his hands earlier had now evaporated.

"Uriel won't talk so maybe you will Michael. I have only one question, are there anymore portals in Heaven's possession?" Death asked.

"None," Michael said plainly.

"How do we know you aren't spitting lies?" War condemned. "The only being capable of placing us in this universe is the Creator himself. Would you like to ask him."

War grunted as a response. "What is your purpose here Archangel?"

"It's a very simple one Death. I'm here for my own, now release her."

The necromantic bonds disappeared from Uriel and the Horseman stepped away. Uriel gave War and Death a nasty look before walking over to her fellow Angel. Michael looked her over to make sure she was fine. "You have what you want now fly away before I pluck you like a pigeon," War said smugly.

Michael held Uriel back from tackling War to the ground and clawing his eyes out. "I would fly away but I'd rather enlist your help." Everybody was shocked by Michael's comment.

"You want our help after what we did? I'm not sure I follow you," War responded.

"I agree with the Red Rider. Besides we should kill them where they stand," Uriel added. Everybody tightened their grip around their weapons as they looked at each other.

"No. The Horsemen have an important role in the coming future," Michael said. Everybody relaxed as they released their weapons. "Accompany us and we will answer all of your questions," Michael told them.

Michael conjured a portal that teleported all of them to an outpost called Aura Lamina. The realm was bright, sunny, and warm. Death's ivory mask gleamed from the sun rays beaming down. Two angels circled above like vultures waiting for their lunch to drop dead. Michael escorted the Horsemen into the temple where other Angels turned and shook in disapproval. The Horsemen have bad blood between Angels and Demons. Death and his siblings have killed both Angels and Demons throughout the centuries. That is why there's such hatred between them all. "What a warm welcome," said Death sarcastically.

"Would you treat us any differently if I or Uriel slaughtered one of your kin?"

"I would treat you differently Michael."

The Archangel raised his head a little bit as he turned to towards Death, "How so?"

"I would kill you, plain and simple. It's the

price you pay!"

"What's the price you'll pay Reaper?" Michael snapped.

The Pale Rider tilted his head, "I don't know but it will be heavy."

Death spoke the truth and he knew it. There's no way that one being can kill so many and yet have no consequence to face. Inside the temple Death and War were told the current situation the Angels were dealing with. "The Ark Of The Covenant has been stolen from us. This band of mercenaries is responsible for the theft." Michael paused for a moment to show brief depictions of the mercenaries in combat.

After the images were shown, a transparent map appeared with two dots on it. "They are known as the Black Fang Clan. The clan has two major strongholds in these realms. We'll have to split up in order to make this quick. War and I will take Silvis while Uriel and Death will take Aviam Planium."

The other three looked at one another and then at Michael. "Is there a problem?"

War curled his lip, "of course there is Angel."

"You haven't convinced us to actually help you in your cause," Death added.

Michael summoned forth something that would prove invaluable to the pale one.

"Does this look familiar to you?" Michael asked.

Death started to move forward, "Where did you find the Book of the Dead?"

"It's amazing what you can find when you simply look." It was a subtle jeer that Michael spat at

Death. He's been searching for that book for a very very long time. Death wanted that book, no, Death needed that book.

"I will help you retrieve the Ark," Death said.

War and Uriel shook their heads in disbelief about the agreement. The four of them split into two teams as stated before and departed for the different realms.

****

The portal tore a hole into the area allowing the beings to access the realm. Michael and War stepped through the portal and took in their surroundings. The forest was like any other but it seemed foreboding. The band of two started down the path so they could reach the stronghold. There was an uneasy silence that saturated the air. "If you have a question you should ask," Michael said.

"Earlier you said we, The Horsemen, have an important part to play in the future. I believe you meant more than just the end-war."

"Yes War you are correct. You and your kin are meant for so much more than just these quests. There is a great power imbued in all four of you," Michael finished.

"Why did you wait until now to tell me this Archangel?" Michael paused before speaking, "I fear what you will become in the future. I fear that more than the power you wield."

The Red Rider grabbed Michael by his foot, "What are you doing War?!"

Michael was pulled out of the air and out of

the path of flying arrows.

"Mercenaries!"

The forest was thick making it difficult to spot their adversaries. War deflected arrow after arrow while Michael was plotting an escape. "War! Cover your eyes!" War did as he was told.

"Solar Light!" It was a defensive spell that emitted a brilliant light that blinded their enemies temporarily.

"Now's our chance, move," said the Angel.

War whistled for his horse that appeared out of a burst of flames. The Rider and the Archangel accelerated down the path in an attempt to elude their enemies.

The two of them evaded arrows left and right as they continued down the path. War dodged a sword-strike from a rival mercenary. "A band of Merc Riders."

War sliced one Fang off his horse and jabbed another. More Fangs appeared out of nowhere and slammed into his steed. The Red Rider engaged in close-quarter-combat. Michael ascended into the sky.

"Where are you going?!" War shouted.

"Have faith Rider," Michael responded.

"In what?" War thought.

They were headed straight for a dead end and would be cornered by the Black Fangs. The two of them could kill them all fairly easily but they didn't have the time. Michael flew above the mountain that blocked the path. Michael placed his hands together, in prayer, and started to speak in a cosmic language that very few know. The heavens parted and a glorious light shined upon the Angel. Then an ugly streak of lightning struck the Angel, empowering him. A mystical glow formed around his hands, now it was time. Michael started to lift the mountain off its very foundation. All who had eyes could witness such power. The floating mountain produced a shadow over the forest and all of its contents. War himself was amazed by the sheer power that was being displayed. It was crazy to think that Michael feared the Four. The Red Rider used the incredible moment to his advantage and broke away from the mercenaries. Chaos galloped faster than he had ever before showing his true speed. Michael proved just how strong he was in being the strongest and the most fit leader of the Hellguard. War and Chaos made their way from underneath the massive floating stone and gained distance. Once Michael knew that War was clear he released the mountain. Anyone and anything that was caught beneath the mountain was completely pulverized into dust. War was launched from his saddle and rolled across the grass until he slid to a stop. "Faith the size of a mustard seed," whispered Michael.

War climbed to his feet and called forth his horse. "A warning next time before you decide to move mountains."

Michael grinned at the Horseman's remark, "of course."

They followed the pathfinder talisman through the woodlands until they found the mercenary stronghold deep in the heart of Silvis. War dismissed Chaos from any further duties as he crouched down. The two of them examined the fortress from afar. "What do you propose for infiltration?" the Angel asked.

"Infiltration? Why don't we just level the fortress instead? The Ark is most likely kept underneath the stronghold."

Michael definitely proved that he was capable of doing just that. "I'm not going to take that kind of risk," Michael replied.

"Have it your way Angel. A head-on assault, no stealth, just carnage so this way it'll be more fun," proposed War.

The Archangel nodded in agreement with the new plan of action. The Horseman leapt from his position and plummeted towards the stronghold like a fatal comet. The impact sent Black Fangs flying in every direction. *Perdition* sliced through his foes swift and clean. Mercenaries fell left and right as War continued to swing with chaotic precision. "Where are you Michael, there won't be any more left by the time I'm done."

As if on cue the Archangel swooped into action. Two of the deadliest warriors fighting back-to-back meant no one was leaving the fortress alive. Archers formed on the walk-ways above and started firing on the intruders below. Michael knocked a few arrows away before he took to the air to clear the walkways. The angelic blade tore through the archers with ease. War on the other hand stuck to the ground-game. He slammed one Fang to the ground and impaled him. War thrived from chaos generated from conflict and at times he would go completely insane. When he entered this animalistic stage, this feral stage, there is no stopping the infamous Red Rider. More mercenaries swarmed around the dreaded Horseman. They tried to overwhelm him but it didn't work in the mercs favor. Flames of mystical fire started to engulf his entire sword.

"Witness the power of Perdition." War jumped into the air and then slammed back down sword-first. All attackers were completely vaporized from the wave of flames produced. Within the ashes Michael could see the very man he would come to fear in the future. Perdition rested on his back once more, "Now that's done let's find that Ark."

The Rider turned the entire fortress upside down looking for the sacred treasure. "Where is that blasted thing?"

Michael closed his eyes and used a spell that allowed him to search the fortress more thoroughly, nothing. "I don't see it either which means it's not here," Michael concluded.

"It's up to the others now," War added.

****

Death and Uriel traversed the desert realm before entering a shallow canyon. Honey-comb like rock structures lined both sides of the canyon. "Very peculiar," Death said staring at the walls. "What was that?" Uriel asked. "I know that you hate me and my brother but I could care less how you feel. All that matters now is the Ark," Death said. "I wouldn't have it any other way," Uriel responded. Death felt a hot-numbing pain in his shoulder and as a side-effect his head became very heavy. "Something wrong don't feel . . . right," he said hunching forward in his saddle. A scorpion the size of a small dog crawled on his back.

Uriel snatched the scorpion off his back and killed it. "Rider are you okay?" Uriel asked. "I'm fine just get out of this canyon before more show up." *Damnation*, Death's scythe, sliced through three scorpions with a single swing. "Get moving," he barked as more crawled out of the honey-combed nests. Echoes, his trusty steed, sped up as Death spurred him. Uriel swayed left and right as scorpions jumped towards her. A few of them latched onto the Archangel. Their venomous tails couldn't penetrate the heavenly-forged armor. She repulsed the creatures by using pure energy. The Pale Rider continued to slice through the scorpions as he rode through the canyon. He hopped into the air slashing through more of the pests as Echoes trampled over others. One scorpion jumped right in front of Death's face but he reacted quickly. The Horseman grabbed the scorpion and squished it with his bare-hand. Rider and horse jumped out of the canyon as the entire colony of scorpions poured out of their nests. Uriel swooped in behind the Rider and conjured an earthquake spell that leveled the entire canyon. The walls and rocks crumbled upon one another until the scorpions were buried alive. A moment later the ground shook once more after the initial earthquake. "After-shock?" Death wondered. "It wasn't a natural earthquake so there can't be an after-shock," Uriel answered. The ground continued to shake as the two of them turned around. A scorpion of colossus proportions emerged from the sand. Death looked over the massive beast, "ladies first." Uriel rolled her eyes before attacking the monster. The Angel assaulted from above as the Pale Rider assaulted from the ground. Death hacked at its legs chipping away the thick skin. The beast acknowledged the annoyance and knocked Death off of his horse and into the hot-dusty sand. "Death!" Uriel called out before being whacked out of the sky by the scorpion's tail. The Archangel streaked through the air like an arrow and slammed into the ground.

Uriel turned over so she could sit up. She was so disoriented that she didn't even realize that the scorpion was rearing back its tail to stab with his stinger. The Angel was in danger and there was only one person who could save her. Death leaped into the air, pulled a fancy move, and severed the scorpion's head. The head and body of the gigantic monster crashed to the ground. "Seems like he knocked you senseless," Death said as he offered help. Uriel slapped his boney hand away and got up on her own. "I've stayed my blade from your throat for the sake of this mission," Death told her. "See me when this is all over," she said boastingly. "Your golden blood was spilled once by my brother War and that was minuscule compared to what I can do."

A necromantic aura formed around his hands as the Archangel and Pale Rider stared each other down. They will definitely be seeing each other later on in the future. Bad blood can never settle peacefully. The tension broke as the ground started to shake once more. "What is that? Another scorpion?" Uriel pondered. "No," Death said pointing into the distance, "Black Fang riders." The battle wasn't long and it proved too much. The stronghold stood amongst the sand and heat waves. The sentry that watched over the gate spotted two distant figures. They were riders that were sent out earlier. As they got closer the sentry noticed that they were dragging something. "Open up we have captives!" one rider yelled. The sentry pulled the lever and activated the gate. The mercenaries passed through and were immediately questioned. "What happened to the others?" one asked. "These two attacked us," the rider said pointing at their captives. Their comrades looked in astonishment. "The Pale Rider and a Archangel. Are they dead?" another mercenary questioned. "No, they are very powerful and the best we could do was overwhelm them," said the other rider.

"Let's shackle the angel before she wakes up. I don't want her to know that we have the Ark, she might get ideas." The two hostages started to wake up. The Black Fangs rushed over to secure them and discovered the truth. The spell faded away and a jagged blade impaled a mercenary. Death was known for his deceptive spells and this was a clear example. He used a spell that disguised him and the Angel. By the time the enemy found out it was too late. Damnation tore through any opposition. Death kicked one merc to the ground, stabbed him, and clipped another. He tossed one man into the air that Uriel slashed through. She dodged arrows fired from archers below. Uriel knocked away arrows before she threw her sword that plowed through mercs. Death would've been cut by her sword if he didn't evade, "careful!" Uriel smirked as she continued to fight. The Horseman sliced through the mercenaries like a bladed-cyclone. Men fell left and right as the Pale Rider continued his onslaught. Death summoned a flock of undead ravens that clawed away at any foe that was left standing. Uriel landed next to her partner, "crows." Death stopped and turned slowly, "ravens." "Whatever you say," said Uriel while she flicked a raven with her wing. The pale man grabbed a deceased mercenary and sat him up-right. "What do you plan to do? Talk to him," Uriel joked.

"Precisely now be quiet," the Rider demanded. Words from an ancient language spewed from underneath his ivory mask. The necromantic aura formed around his hands once more as he placed them against the man's chest. The mercenary was reanimated with life and was startled as he awoke. "Welcome back," Death greeted. The man looked around for a moment before staring at Death. "Why did you bring me back?" the man asked. "You don't deserve to rest," the pale one replied. "Who said anything about rest. How can I rest in a realm of blasting heat and raging flames? At least I have an afterlife." Death wrapped his hand around the mercs throat and slammed him against the wall. The Rider knew exactly what he was talking about. The

Horsemen aren't rewarded with an afterlife. Once their time is up they are casted into a fate much worse than death. "Where's the Ark?!" Death growled as he slammed him against the wall again. "In the cellar low beneath the fortress. I very much doubt that we'll be seeing each other again," the man said. "Don't be so sure of yourself, anything is possible." Death released the necromantic grip he had allowing the man's soul to return to the realm of Hell where it belonged. Uriel used a spell similar to Michael's that allowed her to search the fortress, it was there. She then contacted Michael telepathically, "we've found it get here fast." A portal opened a moment later and the other two stepped through. War and Michael looked around as if déjà vu overcame them. "The Ark?" Michael inquired. "The cellar beneath the fortress," Uriel replied. "Good, very good. War go and bring the Ark up here." War was about to spit his distaste of the order but Death cut him off. "We're going to need him," the Pale Rider said. Michael turned to face Death, "why is that?" The others looked to where the rider pointed. A brigade of mercenaries were advancing towards the stronghold. "You have your Ark. Get out of here before it's taken again," said Death. "Miss out on such a fight? Never," replied Michael. "Finally you're talking some sense," War added. Chaos and Echoes erupted out of clouds of mist and their masters saddled up. "Horsemen first," Uriel gestured. The Pale Rider grinned underneath his mask, "why thank you." War and Death sped through the sand and dust spearheading straight towards the brigade.

Michael and Uriel soared high in the sky and

summoned a powerful spell. The heavens parted and hideous streaks of lightning struck the brigade below. Black Fangs were blown into the sky and other were roasted to the bone. They might be beautiful creatures from divine creation but they do know how to kill and they do it well.

Whenever a Horseman enters conflict their natural eye color spreads out and covers their entire eye. They've come to call it 'combat glaze' and right now their eyes we combat glazed. Death hurtled over the frontline while War plowed straight through. Anyone caught underneath Echoes was crushed. Death hopped off his horse and engaged the mercenaries. They weren't the filthy animals like the Orcs but they weren't any better either. Death swung in wide-greedy arcs and horizontal chops that were devastating. He utilized the full-length of Damnation to keep the Black Fangs at bay. War's approach was much more different. He remained on his red horse as he chopped away. The height advantage left the opposing combatants hopelessly outmatched. War swung so hard that one of the mercenary's head actually cracked. Chaos reared back to kick mercenaries away. War bounded from his saddle and plunged into combat sword-first. Perdition slammed into the ground and sharp slabs of rock protruded from the ground and impaled anyone in the effective radius. The heavy blade of War's sword completely destroyed any opposition. The mercenaries didn't stand a chance but they continued to come. "They must want a swift death, well come then!" the Red Rider roared. The two riders slaughtered the Black Fangs like they were cattle. This was nothing but a cosmic lifetime of combat and killing that was burned into their very souls; Death and War were taking on the brigade single-handedly.

The Angels didn't even dare to intervene. "They look like lions amongst lambs. They're actually enjoying themselves, what animals." Michael wagged his finger at Uriel, "choose your words more carefully." He floated forward a little bit. "Animals swing and fight wildly. The Horsemen are ancient beings that have seen millenniums of war and conflict. Their combat mastery is perfect and senses are incredible as well." "You admire them," Uriel realized. "They were created before Angels and Demons. There is definitely something we can learn from them. What we see now is only a prequel of their true hidden power. I pray when that day comes we are all prepared."

That day and threat wasn't near but a different threat was approaching. Massive scorpions like the one Death and Uriel faced before had showed up. There were three of them that were being used as transport for other troops. "The brigade was just a warm up," said War. "Horsemen!" Michael called from above. The two Riders looked up to see what he was going to say. "Me and Uriel will take the two scorpions on the outside while you take the one in the middle." The Horsemen nodded as the Angels flew towards the scorpions.

Uriel performed a spiral move that deflected

arrows. She swooped underneath the scorpion and then back into the air. Uriel's sword coursed with lightning and then she threw it. The sword pierced through the scorpion and ultimately killed it. Michael twirled his sword whipping energy waves at the other scorpion. The beast was sliced apart by the energy waves as they were unleashed. The scorpion toppled to the sizzling ground to never move again. Michael's tempered fury returned back behind the calm exterior he usually portrays. Two of the colossal beasts have been dealt with by the Archangels. It was up to the Horsemen to finish the fight. Death and War zipped underneath the scorpion and slashed away at the legs. The scorpion became frustrated and tried to stab them with its tail. War dodged the tail and then struck it loosening the stinger. The archers that were posted on top started to fire explosive arrows. Explosions bombarded the Horsemen and even blew Death from his saddle. Dust was kicked up in his face impairing his vision temporarily. The Pale Rider retrieved his scythe as he came to his senses. "Death!" a voice shouted. War blasted through the dust and scooped his brother. "You owe me one Death." He patted War on his shoulder, "I'll pay you back soon." They narrowly dodged a few arrows, "how soon?" "Now!" Death said to War as he leaped from the horse. Death planted his scythe vertical to the leg, swung around the haft twice, and then launched himself to the top of the scorpion. Damnation split in two smaller scythes with large and equally potent blades. He flipped one merc off the scorpion and proceeded to kill two more. Death stooped low to dodge an arrow and the slammed his blades into a man's chest. The Rider tossed one more merc into a group that fell off the back of the scorpion. Death threw another merc by his scythes before turning his attention to the creature. The two individual scythes came together to form Damnation and targeted the tail. He tossed his scythe slicing through the tail causing it to detach. Death ran forward, jumped, caught the stinger and threw it into the scorpion's back. Damnation slapped back into his palm and he then slammed into the stinger driving it through the scorpion. Green slime and goo gushed from the wound as the beast crashed into the ground and died.

The Pale Rider stood up from the dirt as his brother approached. War looked over Death's shoulder to the fallen beast. "Not bad but I would've done it a different way," War examined. "What would you have done War?" Ripped his head off," he replied simply. Michael and Uriel descended out of the sky carrying the Ark. "You have what you came for, is it fine?" Death asked.

"Perfectly so, thanks to you two," Michael said. The Ark of the Covenant burned into a white-hot orb and returned to Heaven. "Just do me a favor Horsemen," Michael started, "don't kill anything for a while." The combat glaze faded away from their eyes. "I'm not doing anything for a few centuries," War responded as he stretched. The Archangels started to fly towards their portal. "Uriel," Death called. She turned around in mid-air. "Try not to hold a grudge so things will go more smoothly next time," Death finished. "I hope there won't be a next time," she said before flying through the portal. Death and Uriel finally agreed on something. "I don't know about you brother but I'm going home," War said. "The same for me," replied Death. War disappeared through his portal and returned to his realm. Death mounted Echoes and activated a portal for home. He felt around for a moment and found a gift. "The Book Of The Dead. So he didn't forget after all." The Pale Rider was going to be busy for a very long time. Good thing he is immortal.

Cold, Cold Fury

Serenity looked at her spear as she rode down the snow-covered path. Her black steed trotted and snorted as the warrior headed to her destination. Snow-flakes fell while Serenity continued to summon a flame enchantment. Flame enchantments allowed Serenity to use magical fire either through her weapon or her hands. Every time she tried flames would begin to form until they died altogether. "Why is this happening? I'm a Horseman for Christ sake I should be able to do this." The phantom horse simply snorted in response to her master, "Thanks Cinder." Serenity was unable to summon the enchantment so she searched for one who could. The master of magic and spells lingered somewhere deep in a cave. It is said that the cave is protected by stone guardians. Something that would be easy work for a Horseman such as herself. Her deep bordeaux colored hair continued to gather snow as she looked to the mountain. That was her true destination, not the cave. There was a barrier that she couldn't get pass without the help of the hermit. The Horseman and steed finally arrived at the cave to find the entrance guarded by two large statues. The large statues looked strange with a short snout and wicked teeth. Serenity dismounted Cinder and inspected the entrance. A thick slab of stone was the door with ancient markings on it. The stone was very hard to cut or smash. Serenity could probably conjure a spell that would bypass the door but it would take too long. "Any ideas Cinder?" The Horseman turned around to see her trusty sidekick had vanished. "Oh," Serenity said to herself. One way or another she had to find a way in. Her pink eyes glazed over signaling approaching conflict. Serenity rolled to her left dodging one hammer and leaped backwards dodging another hammer. The colossus statues were alive and thirsty for blood. They're about to learn that Serenity doesn't bleed so easily. The stone guardians roared out of irritation and their inability to hit their target. Serenity summoned her spear and pointed at the giant stone monsters. "My turn," the warrior said. The Horseman rushed forward as the guardians stood firm in the midst of combat.

She directed a hammer strike into the ground before slashing at its shin. That guardian stumbled back as the other one advanced. The guardian swung its heavy hammer meeting its opponent. Serenity blocked the heavy blow but was still knocked backwards. She slid through the snow before coming to a halt. Her eyes narrowed before she unleashed a flurry of mystic-pink energy waves that slammed into the guardian. This specific attack utilized raw energy in a wave form to destroy its intended target. The stone menace was dazed, confused and open for attack.

The Black Rider, Serenity, bounded through the air and brought down a vertical chop that sliced clean through the monster's head. The guardian crashed to the ground and crumbled into jagged pieces of rock. The other guardian started to swing wildly at the rider. Serenity easily dodged the attacks before retaliating with rapid swipes and jabs that caused the giant to fall. She then threw her spear that knocked the hammer out of the stone beast's hand into the air. The Horseman then caught the hammer mid-flight and brought it down on the guardian's head, this time the head exploded. Serenity tossed the hammer away while the body crumbled away like the first. "Not so tough," Serenity jeered. Snow permeated the piles of rock soaking them. Two more added to her very extensive body count. The massive door of wet stone began to shine as it rose off the ground. "It must have been something I said." Serenity placed the shrunken spear on her back and started to walk through the long cave.

The cave wasn't of natural formation at all. The walls were perfectly rounded and smooth with markings on them. The ancient words and symbols that glowed provided all the light she needed. The cave that the Horseman at first thought was endless revealed a second door. This one was much smaller than the first but twice as thick. This door too rose like the first but the sight was different this time around. There was nothing but candles that lined the room on both sides leading towards the hermit's study. At the table sat the underling himself. He resembled a ram in the face with horns to match. His face was rather flat and hard and riddled with age. He was older than the Horsemen themselves and definitely had the knowledge to prove it. His white hair was shoulder length and a little bit curly as well. The robes he wore were as old as the mage and the once vibrant red color was now a dark maroon. Ancient, that's the word that best describes the conjurer. His greasy lips formed into a grin as Serenity stood in his presence. "What is this? One of the Four amongst me." Serenity crossed her arms, "Yes Hermit I need your help once more." Hermit moved from his seat as he neared Serenity with an abnormal gait. "I always favored your company the best out of your siblings, do you know why?" Serenity shrugged her shoulders before he continued. Hermit brushed her hair behind her ear, "You're so much more pleasant than your brothers." Serenity smiled, "I can be cruel just like them too." She gripped his long white beard with her claws and began to pull. Hermit slapped her hand away, "Enough! What is it that you seek Horseman?" She pulled her spear from her back but it remained in its shrunken form. When the spear was in its shrunken form it was easier to carry. "I need a fire enchantment so I can destroy the barrier between me and that portal."

Hermit took the spear, "Ah yes *Sorrows* how long has it been since we've met, a millennium?" Serenity rolled her eyes, "Can you do it?" "Of course I can," Hermit said offendedly. "But Horseman you know my services come with a price." "Oh? I almost forgot after dealing with your stone fools. So what will it be this time what must I fetch?" Serenity asked. Hermit smirked, "Nothing to fetch but instead a crucible." He handed *Sorrows* back to the Black Rider. "A crucible of what?" the Rider asked. "Of your will." A burning sensation subtlety grew until it pierced through her head as her eyes filled with fire. Serenity clutched *Sorrows* in one hand and her own head in the other hand. She knotted her jaw as the sensation increased for she dared not to yell out in pain. Everything around her vanished as she slowly fell out of consciousness.

The worn marble floor started to collect dust as the Horseman laid there. Her head started to clear as she got to her feet. She brushed her hair to get rid of any dust that was trapped within. "That foolish mage just made me very mad," she said to herself. A mage is a person who has a deep understanding of magic. Serenity noticed the draft in the air and quickly realized where she stood. It was a floating platform composed of some ceramic rock and there were more like it. They were all suspended in the air by some invisible force. In the distance was the largest one of them all, it was actually an arena. That platform had large arching pillars that all met at the top. If there was any destination it would be over there. The smaller platforms were easy to reach since it only took a single jump. Serenity almost overshot a platform due to poor-judgement. Good thing she had claws in place of her regular nails. She pulled herself up and took a moment to more carefully analyze her next step. The arena was right in front of her but it was also the furthest distance. Serenity held *Sorrows* that collected explosive energy in its blade. It was going to be like using lounging stick ready to explode. "Here goes my sane reasoning." She took three steps forward before slamming the blade into the platform blasting her upward. The platform of ceramic rock exploded into a million pieces as the Horseman soared through the dank air. The large platform became nearer and nearer as she continued to fly. Serenity latched onto a pillar and slid around it before plummeting to the floor. A small crater was left where she landed with cracked and uprooted slabs of rock. Fat clouds of dust floated around the Horseman. A dark figure lingered in the clouds of dust unbeknownst to the Horseman. The figure lashed out and struck Serenity. She rolled across the floor from the extreme force of the hit. Her eyes glazed over as she grabbed *Sorrows.* The figure stepped into the light.

"It can't be!" The attacker was Serenity but a different version, a more twister version, a darker version. She was cladded in black armor that was ornate and composed of advanced plating, synthetic fibers, and magic. A small crown rested on her head and tattoos could be seen on her face and shoulders. The tattoos covered her entire pale body but only a few could be seen. Serenity took another hard hit across the face, this time by *Sorrows*. This spear, like its wielder, completely altered. The spearhead was longer and twice as sharp with a second smaller spearhead on the bottom end of the haft, the handle of the spear. Heavy magic not only surged in the spear and armor but through the Dark Rider as well. The drastic change in appearance could only mean one thing, broken seal. The seventh seal has to be broken in order for the apocalypse armor and weapon to be acquired. Serenity looked upon her inverted self in both shock and amazement. She always knew that the Horsemen had great power but nothing like this. Serenity could feel the raw power as if invisible waves passed over her. The Dark Rider marched forward menacingly with the spear in her right hand and magic forming in the left. She raised her hand and discharged an incredible blast of magic. Serenity countered with a blast of her own and the collision caused the arena to shake. Clouds of dust hung in the air as the two Riders stared each other down from the opposite ends. It was about to get very ugly!

Serenity blocked the attack with *Sorrows*. Even the attacks were stronger, amplified by the power of the seals. The Dark Rider was fast too, extremely fast. All of her attacks blended together. It was impossible to tell a swipe from a slash. She was also alternating between forehand and backhand grip. It was about to be a tough fight and Serenity already knew that. Since Serenity was fighting herself that would mean her double would have the same flaws. The Black Rider tends to leave her left side open during combat and her doppelgänger was doing the same. Serenity blocked a few hits before delivering a solid thrust. The doppelgänger pivoted to the right and slashed Serenity across her back. She should've known that her twin figured out a counterpoint for the flaw. "I guess I'll use everything up my sleeve for this one," Serenity said aloud. She dodged another attack before the Black Rider delivered an upward slash. The doppelgänger flipped through the air before landing on her feet. Serenity followed up with two sizzling magic blasts before dealing a solid kick. The Dark Rider struck Serenity hard in the stomach causing her to double over. The evil twin then sliced the Horseman across the face. The Black Rider recovered quickly and casted a spell that fired shards of stone towards her adversary.

The Dark Rider blocked with her spear before evading. "I'm not finished yet!" shouted Serenity. She fired a volley of magic blasts before slashing her twin opponent multiple times. The altered version was rocked by the violent and viscous combo that left her dazed momentarily. Serenity finished the doppelgänger with and explosive thrust. The Apocalyptic Serenity, the evil version, laid in front of the Black Rider defeated. The dark twin spoke in the Nephilim native language. "The end of days is upon you and no one will suffer more than you and your brothers." Before Serenity could ask any questions, the corpse started to shake before a white light erupted from its center mass. The intense light exploded into a blinding flash. Serenity found herself back in the Hermit's study. The mage loomed over her with a devilish grin. "I see your will has not been broken after all," Hermit said. Serenity shot up and punched the mage square across his face and into a book shelf. A few scrolls and books fell as Serenity choked the ram-headed underling. "No but I'll break you. If you don't want to visit my brother you best grant me the fire enchantment." "Fine, just let me go," Hermit pleaded. Serenity threw Hermit by his horns and waited. Hermit got to his hooves and commenced his job. Moments later the spearhead of *Sorrows* was engulfed in a pinkish flame. "Are you satisfied Black Rider?" She pointed her flaming spear at the mage. "If you ever do that again I will subject your soul to some of the worst pain ever," the Horseman warned. "You witnessed something unfavorable?" Hermit asked. Serenity stopped at the entrance, "Favorable or unfavorable it is inevitable." *Sorrows* shrunk to its smaller size as it was placed on her back. Serenity saw her future self-cladded in the Apocalypse Armor. The speed, the strength, the power, it was incredible but frightening. It was a true challenge to go against such an opponent. She nearly exhausted her magic in combat and now it needs time to restore itself. Serenity mounted her onyx steed and trotted off towards the mountain.

Snowflakes fell before her eyes as she headed for the objective. It tickled her a little bit. It's the thought that even the smallest of things has a duty or a purpose. The snowflake for example is an everyday concurrence but it has a purpose. Each snowflake has a unique design that can only be crafted by the Creator himself and yet it has a rather pointless end. It falls from the out-of-reach heavens, through the sky, and then shatters on the ground. Such an interesting beginning that only leads to such a disappointing end. Serenity thought about that and will forever use that as motivation. Whenever she feeling tired or feel like she's pointless or has meaningless purpose she'll remember the snowflake.

As she road down the path Serenity tried to summon the enchantment through her hands. Moments later her hands sparked and flames erupted. It was an uncanny feeling of wielding both life and destruction in one's hands. The fire had a tiny heartbeat, faint but precious and something very important. Something that gave man warmth in their darkest hours and help improve their lives. Yet at the same time it was pure destruction that could burn down homes, incinerate a man to his knees, annihilate an entire habitat. Its purpose depended on how it was used. It's very uncanny but what's normal to a Horseman? Destruction and carnage, that's normal to a Horseman. That'll never change for eons to come. Cinder seemed uneasy as they moved through the valley. Her horse was sensing something from the 'beyond,' something dead. Serenity didn't notice yet so she just thought it was the wind. "Calm down girl it's just a little breeze." Serenity patted Cinder on her neck as they continued on their quest. Only if she knew that there were spirits in the woods. Serenity thought about earlier when her steed was unsettled. "Nothing easily spooks Cinder so there has to be something wrong?" she thought. The Black Rider looked into the woods and stared. The longer she stared the more she could clearly see the spirits. Serenity could feel that they weren't the peaceful kind.

They were damned souls, lost and forgotten crying for vengeance. The spirits were wrapped in torn, tattered robes. Some had their faces hidden underneath hoods and masks. The ones that didn't wear masks or hoods wore a scarred face. What was left of the face anyway, gashed, clawed, cut, torn, and severed. Whatever happened to them, they didn't deserve it. One of them noticed the strange person and reacted. The spirit stared back with a piercing gaze that ripped through her mind. It was like a very thin needle hitting the middle of the forehead passing clean through to the back. Serenity never felt such hatred trapped in one being. "What happened to them?" she wondered. The Horseman held her head as Cinder came to a stop. The phantom horse let out a whiny as she reared back. Serenity was nearly thrown from her saddle. She let go of the reins and grabbed Cinder's mane. Serenity then forcefully pushed Cinder back down and regained control.

"What is wrong with you!"

Cinder was calmer but breathing heavily. No matter what the Horseman did her steed wouldn't take another step. Serenity looked up to see the foregone city on the side of the mountain. It was once a marvel but now it was a disappointment. She hopped off of Cinder and let her steed disappear into a cloud of smoke.

Serenity entered the city and looked around. It was home to scholars and knowledge seekers. A place where many from across the realms would come to quench their thirst for intellect. Death, Serenity's older brother, one time visited the city in search of more scrolls and books on necromancy. Necromancy generally deals with communicating with the dead. The Pale Rider was by far the greatest necromancer ever seen. Death can summon entire groups of undead souls to do his bidding if he desires. The number of spells that Death knows outweighs his body count. That's saying something since his body count was in the millions. Death, like the rest of the Horsemen, has been living for thousands of years. Most of those years they've been fighting in battles and wars. The Horsemen learned many lessons over the years and perfected their fighting styles. They are among the most revered killers in all the realms. The only one close to Death's body count was War. Serenity killed plenty of beasts and creatures but none were as satisfying as Demons. Demons were vial beasts that came in all shapes and sizes. They originate from the black pits of Hell.

The Black Rider hated Demons just because. If she could go on a personal crusade to purge them from the universe, she would. The only thing that keeps her at bay is the pact that they all signed. The Angels crafted the pact so there would be an official and formal truce between the tree parties. Angels were crafty creatures themselves. She didn't enjoy killing Angels but she has killed plenty of them too. If they were in her way they died, plain and simple. Whatever the job was the Horsemen would get it done. Shadows zipped pass Serenity as she walked through the city. They were the same spirits from earlier in the woods. The spirits lined the roofs of the buildings and they lined the streets as well. She really couldn't see their faces but she could sense the hostility. Serenity pulled her spear from her back as her eyes glazed over. The spirits pounced on the Horseman all at once in an attempt to kill her. Serenity blew every last one of them back with an energy repulse. The energy repulse is a powerful out-blast of energy that emits from the person's body. The spirits were slammed into the walls and ground. *Sorrows* ripped through three vengeful wraiths, or ghosts, before destroying another. Serenity lashed out at one spirit but he was clever. He phased through the Horseman and slammed her on the ground. Serenity rolled back onto her feet and vanquished five more spirits with a single slice. One wraith slammed into her as another knocked her into a wall. Serenity went through the wall causing it to crumble on top of her. Now she was mad. Serenity sprung from the waste and fired energy blasts at the enemy. Her attacks were swift and lethal that purged countless spirits. It wasn't good enough since more kept coming. She wouldn't keep fighting the wraiths that way because would take too long. Serenity leaped into the sky as she summoned her fire enchantment.

The spearhead started to boar flames as she came plummeting back towards the ground. The Black Rider crashed down unleashing a shock-wave of flames that eradicated everything in its path. Buildings fell, the roads were upturned, and the spirits disappeared. Don't mess with the Black Rider. Everything was scorched and set ablaze. Serenity placed *Sorrows* on her back and continued her journey. The walk to the cave was a lengthy one but it wasn't impossible. She didn't want to call Cinder because of her behavior earlier. Dealing with an unruly beast is a waste of time. She finally reached the cave along with its obstacle. The entrance was frozen solid, a wall of ice that was a few feet thick. Fire started to form in Serenity's hands. She moved towards the entrance, placed her hands on the ice and turned up the heat. The ice slowly started to melt as flames licked at the frozen wall. Serenity increased the temperature so the flames burn even hotter. As the wall was slowly seared away Serenity noticed something. This ice was melting a lot slower than normal ice, 'normal' ice. That meant the barrier of ice was made of magic. So the questioned remained, what created the wall?

The ice exploded and knocked the Rider to the bitter-cold ground. Her eyes became combat glazed as the source of the explosion revealed itself. A massive dragon emerged from the cave seething with rage. The incredible beast stretched out her neck and roared. The dragon moved forward menacingly and stepped right in front of the Horseman. "Who disturbs Gelida Draco," she said in a booming voice. She dipped down to look at Serenity. "One of the Four stands before me? How expected." "Speak sense Draco you knew I was coming?" Serenity asked. "Not you exactly but I knew one of the Riders would be at my door step. It was only a matter of time since I guard that." Draco pointed at the portal with a crooked smile revealing her razor sharp teeth. "I will destroy that portal and you too Draco if you stand in my way." Draco laughed, "And why is it you seek the portal?" "It leads to Earth and that's forbidden. It upsets the balance you know that," Serenity replied. "Ah and keep it you shall. The reason why the Horsemen were created, to maintain balance. To safe guard the equilibrium of the universe," Draco finished. "Enough of this I'm done talking," Serenity said. She started walking towards the portal before she was stopped. "I can't allow you to destroy that portal," the dragon told her. "I wasn't asking." She fired a lethal blast of energy that slapped the dragon's face. Draco rubbed her scaly cheek before she dropped down to all fours. "You will regret that Rider." The dragon lashed out with an angry growl.

Serenity dodged the savage tail with a combat roll before attacking again. *Sorrows* slashed the dragon across her front legs and face. Draco became enraged and unleashed a flurry of swipes and chops. Serenity evaded the flurry easily but never saw the ice beam coming. The sub-zero beam hit the Black Rider center mass and froze her solid. Draco laughed heavily as she examined her new ice sculpture. "What a beautiful piece of art. You will be a great edition to my collection." Before Draco could obtain the frozen trophy she began to shake. The dragon backed away as she felt a growing heat. "What is this?!" she growled. Serenity exploded from the ice blazing hot. "I am your end," the Horseman told her. Serenity fired a chaotic stream of mystic fire at the beast that roared from the pain. "Enough!" Draco bellowed. The dragon shot into the sky above and descended back down like a frozen comet. Serenity was quick and timed it perfectly. She dodged the shockwave with a jump and then placed her spear into Draco's head. She then grabbed her tail and with extraordinary strength hurled the dragon into the side of the mountain. Draco shook off the attack. "You will not kill me Horseman." Gileda Draco flipped forward and whipped her tail down. The sheer force threw Serenity from the dragon's lair and over the side of the mountain. The Rider fell uncontrollably through the air with the ground coming closer every second. The frozen beast swooped from above and grabbed Serenity in her talons. "I no longer want you in my collection I just want you dead!" Draco roared.

Freezing air rushed pass the two of them as they fell. The dragon slashed Serenity which caused her to crash into the city street. A large cloud of dust and snow was thrown into the air due to the impact. Draco used her wings to flush away the cloud. She was pleased to see the sight of a weakened Horseman. "What's wrong Rider are you hurt," she said smugly. Serenity coughed up some blood as she waited. The dragon leaned very low over the wounded Black Rider. "Don't worry it won't last much longer." Serenity discharged a blast of fire so she could vanish. The beast clawed at her eyes from the pain of the fire. "I will have your head Serenity I swear it!" The Black Rider was in terrible condition and she needed to finish the beast. Draco regained her vision and began to search for the Horseman. "Where are you Nephilim!" Gelida demanded. "Here!" Serenity leaped from the roof of a building and slashed Draco across her face with a flaming spearhead. She cried out in pain since both of her eyes were sliced and singed closed. Serenity then formed a fiery whip and lassoed the winged beast. The whip melted into Draco's throat as she started to panic. Serenity yanked the whip and pulled her head into a building.

The Black Rider mounted the beast as she struggled to maintain her grip. "I will end us both," Draco said. The massive dragon shot into the sky once more but went even higher. Serenity lost her grip and slipped from her mounted position and was then hanging by a thread. Draco soared ever higher in an attempt to dislodge the Black Rider permanently. It was now or never. The spearhead of *Sorrows* was covered in flames once more and thrusted into frozen flesh. Draco jerked from the fatal strike and slowly started descending. The massive beast crashed into the ground announcing her arrival. She laid on the snow covered ground breathing heavily. The bloody and beaten Horseman stood before the fallen dragon. "You should've gotten out of my way," Serenity said. "There will always be those who will stand against you, order, law, and balance." Bluish blood poured from her hideous wounds. "It won't matter for in the end you, the Horsemen, will defeat your own purpose." "What? You aren't making any sense," Serenity responded. "You'll see," she said with an evil grin. Serenity stabbed Draco in her head finishing her off. She then fired a concentrated energy beam that destroyed the bridge between the two worlds. Serenity dropped to her knees as Cinder emerged to help her master. The Black Rider managed to mount her steed and open a portal that led to her home. "It's going to take time for me to heal." Cinder let out a whiny before they vanished into the portal. Serenity was done . . . for now.

Smoke Him Out!

"My lord there is the flagship," the admiral alerted. Lazarus looked over the specifications of the ship. "I see it Turrok. Get to Sera as fast as you can. I'll take care of *Summer's Dawn.*" "How?" the admiral was very puzzled. Within the specifications it was stated that the ship's armor was heavily reinforced with some kind of classified material. The attack squadrons were being arranged for battle. Cat entered her Y-winged star fighter that had her rank displayed in gold on the wings. Her task was simple, provide air support and relieve the city of enemy forces. "Are you sure about this Lazarus? *Summer's Dawn* is a dreadnaught after all." The massive ventral doors parted to reveal the raging space battle. Chevalier Assault Ships were taking heavy fire and knight attack squadrons were dwindling. It was a losing battle they had to win. "Use the existing debris as cover Cat. I'll take care of the fighters and *Summer's Dawn.* You just worry about Sera," Lazarus told her.

Lazarus rocketed from the bay and towards the flagship. Cat and her attack squadron maneuvered through the debris fields and headed straight for Sera. Lightning bolts destroyed the enemy fighters with brilliant explosions. The star fighters were nimble but they couldn't match the size of a man's body. Lazarus grabbed one star fighter and threw it into another oncoming star fighter. "I can't shake them they're all over me!" Lazarus swooped in behind the enemy fighters and took them out. "Thanks for the assist," the pilot said. He barrel-rolled and continued the fight. Mercy looked at the floating man in space. "Reroute all power and destroy Lazarus!" The Firstborn dodged blast after blast as *Summer's Dawn* continued to fire. One plasma round hit its mark. Everybody on the bridge looked up in awe to see if the divine Lazarus was actually vanquished. "Is he dead?" an operator asked. His answer came with two streaks of lightning striking close to the bridge. "Kill him!" Mercy growled. Lazarus dodged more plasma rounds as he flew around to the back of the dreadnaught. Lazarus zeroed in on the repulsers, the ship's engines, and fired another streak of lightning. The repulsers were protected by energy shields that reflected the attack back. The swift Firstborn smacked his own blast upwards and out of sight. "Great, looks like an inside job," he said to himself. Lazarus zipped through space with one goal in mind. He fired a beam of concentrated energy that was strong enough to overload the energy shields.

The King used the opportunity to punch through the ship's hull and gain access to the inside. NGO soldiers were sucked out into the vacuum where their screams couldn't be heard. Red strobe lights flashed throughout the bridge. "What was that?" Mercy barked. "It was Lazarus sir, he has breached the ship's hull." Mercy was not pleased at all. "Lock down the entire deck no one in or out." The operators pressed buttons on their holo-pads in a coded sequence. "Sir," an operator called. Mercy walked over, "what is it?" "Lazarus isn't headed for the bridge." "Well where is he going?" said Mercy puzzled.

One soldier's chest was crushed as the other one was blasted through the bulkhead door. "So weak" Lazarus taunted. Through the destroyed bulkhead were the blistering fusion reactors. "SOL Mercy SOL." Lazarus fired a single lightning bolt that demolished the reactors. The flag ship let out a loud moan as it lost its mobility. Lazarus blasted through the hull once more and marveled at his work. Mercy grabbed the object nearest to him and cursed angrily. "I can't wait to kill Lazarus." "That's the least of your worries sir," an operator said. *Summer's Dawn* started to fall out of orbit and plummeted towards the planet below. "Reroute all power and head straight for Sera," Mercy ordered. The operators did as commanded while the entire bridge shook uncontrollably and systems sparked. Lazarus traced the dreadnought's trajectory and knew exactly what Mercy was doing. "Oh you fiend." Lazarus flew towards the ship as it entered the planet's thick atmosphere. *Summer's Dawn* turned into a spearhead of flames as did Lazarus due to passing through the atmosphere. The heat was extreme and scorched the ship's already damaged hull. Lazarus' armor became scorched like the ship and his cape disintegrated into ashes. The powerful being flew to the nose of the ship and attempted to change its course. "This scrap metal is heavy!" Lazarus couldn't get the ship to change course or slow down. "I need to stop this ship." He slipped from the ship's nose and flew pass to Chevalier. There was only one thing he could do.

Meanwhile, the lead star fighter dodged the incoming laser bolts and looped behind the enemy fighter. One shot and the enemy bird was gone. Cat's eye caught two more that were pursuing one of her own pilots. "This is Echo 5 I need support!" Cat was already behind them taking pot shots. "Bank right 5," Cat said. The pilot did as commanded causing one hostile fighter to bank too wide. Cat fired a missile that took out the NGO fighter. "One down one to go," she said to herself.

The Commander circled around a few buildings before she obliterated the other enemy fighter. "Thanks for the assist Commander, Echo 5 out." The knight star fighter pulled up and out of the corridors of buildings and disappeared into the chaotic sky battle. Cat tapped on her holo-pad as she checked the battle updates. The city's defenses were up and taking out any hostile threats in the air. With the combined strength of the air defense system and the allied star fighters in the sky they should be able to win this battle. High powered laser bolts slammed into her shields. Another NGO fighter chased Cat through the corridors of buildings and skyscrapers. "Not today fool." She jammed the rudder forward and pulled the stick back. This maneuver caused the pilot to lose temporary control of her star fighter but gain the advantage. Only the most skilled or the insane could pull this trick off. Cat leveled out behind the rival fighter and blasted it out of the sky.

A faint figure shot through high up in the open air. It couldn't have been any bigger than a man. Cat looked to see where the figure was flying from and that's when she saw the mass of blazing metal. "I'll let Lazarus take care of that problem," she said in bewilderment. Lazarus flew a couple more miles pass the city before he came to a stop. His hell-fire eyes scanned over the descending dreadnaught as well over the capitol city. Over ten billion lives counted on the Firstborn. "Time to show real power." The world around him seemed to fluctuate and distort as the power he needed surged through his body. Lazarus blasted through the air and towards *Summer's Dawn.* He was flying so fast that the air couldn't get out of the way. Air particles condensed around his waist as he gained even more speed. Pow! One sonic boom. Everybody inside the city watched as the magnificent figure quickly approached. Pow!

A second sonic boom. Glass shattered from sheer force. Anyone in the radius of the boom were knocked down and left breathless. Cat lost control of her star fighter and nearly crashed from the sonic boom. Glass continued to shatter and break as the Firstborn blew pass. Pow! A third sonic boom. It was powerful enough to level a few buildings. *Summer's Dawn* was closing in on the city.

"Ten miles out." The operator wiped sweat from his forehead. "Sir we have an object fast approaching." Mercy looked at the screen as Lazarus sped towards them. "Brace for impact!!!" Pow! A fourth sonic boom. The two forces met and shock waves exploded from the collision. The city trembled from the clash of god and machine. The deafening sound could be heard throughout the city.

The burning dreadnaught slowed down significantly but it was still moving. Lazarus didn't have the leverage to stop the mechanical beast. *Summer's Dawn* continued downward until the ground crushed beneath his feet. Seeing the grotesque space craft closing in on the city Knight soldiers did what they could to evacuate all civilians in the immediate area. They couldn't save them all but they could minimize casualties. People ran in fear and terror as they were directed away by the Knight soldiers. The leverage was there now and all he had to do was stop it. The metal crunched and squealed as Lazarus increased his grip. Every muscle in his body bulged from the extraordinary stress and pressure. The ones who were held in place by fear watched in amazement as one man wrestled with the metal monster. "Half-mile to the city," he said to himself. Lazarus summoned whatever strength that was left and slammed the smoldering mass of machine to the ground. Citizens and soldiers cheered and celebrated to see that they and the city were saved. Lazarus dropped to his knees completely drained of energy. A star fighter landed and Cat rushed over to check on the king. "Are you okay?" she asked. Lazarus waved his commander away. "Don't waste your time on me Cat. Search the ship for Mercy. Smoke him out!"

Cat nodded before she started issuing orders. "This is the commander to all knight ground forces. Form a perimeter around *Summer's Dawn* and prepare for infiltration." Knight star fighters took care of any stragglers left in the sky as Knight Assault Ships made their way through the clouds. Hours later the ground forces formed the isolation zone around the still smoking dreadnaught. The ship was scanned to see what was left on the inside. Any threats were painted in red and high valued targets where painted in gold. Cat looked over the scans and nodded her head solemnly, "good work." She patted the operator on his back before she walked to the King's tent. Knight soldiers sat on an Armored Personnel Carrier, or A.P.C., that Cat walked passed. "Heard about that aerial battle early ma'am. How many did you take out?" one soldier asked. "I lost track after 50," she said with a grin. The soldiers looked at one another impressed by the commander's skills. Cat waved at them as she proceeded to her destination. The royal guards saluted the high ranking Firstborn as she saluted back and entered the tent. The inside of the tent was filled with hi-tech equipment and systems that were placed all around the tent. The cloth was made out of unique fibers that were as strong the hull of *Oblivion's Edge*, Lazarus' flagship. Lazarus sat behind his desk with his head bowed.

His battle armor was removed and was currently being refurbished as was his cape. So in the meantime he was draped in royal robes of elegant colors. The sudden blaze of hell-fire red eyes would have shocked anybody but Cat was used to it. Lazarus attempted to stand but was still recovering from overexerting himself. Cat moved around to help but Lazarus stopped her. "I know you can't help yourself Cat but try." She sat down on his desk in front of him. Lazarus looked her up and down like a predator scanning his prey. Cat saw the look in his eyes and knew it all too well. "I know you can't help yourself but try," Cat said. Lazarus simply huffed as a response. "What's the status on your operation?" he asked. "My men are moving into the ship and searching for Mercy as we speak." A loud explosion sounded outside the tent. Lazarus looked at the commander, "They're searching huh." Cat sighed at the comment and ran outside to assess the situation. Soldiers moved about scrambling to contain the site. Cat grabbed one and pulled him near. "What happened?" asked Cat. "It's Mercy, he and his men are on the offensive." The iron grip was released and the soldier went about his business.

Cat summoned her scythe before leaping into the newly formed hole on the side of the ship. Laser bolts and plasma bolts shot back and forth like cars on a highway. By the plasma bolts she could tell that her men were firing from the right. She poked her head out to see Mercy and his men firing on her men. The dual-wielding sharpshooter took down an entire platoon using his magnums. Mercy's infamous dual magnums were the most powerful handguns in the galaxy. Cat activated her helmet and plasma-edged scythe. Cat's scythe originally a farm tool but she talked to Zeno about optimizing it for combat. The scythe became Cat's main weapon of choice. Her movement was swift and quick as she hopped over the railing towards Mercy. She sliced through his NGO marauders with ease. The savage marauders were a specialized military division that Mercy formed under the New Galactic Order. They were the main force that Mercy used in his military operations. As soon as the last man dropped a barrage of laser bolts made a frontal assault. "Look who came out to play." Mercy dodged the horizontal chop, balanced on the railing, and continued to shoot. "I didn't know Lazarus let you out of your cage." Cat sliced the railing in two as Mercy jumped and stuck to the wall. "I'm seen as an equal to Lazarus and he treats me as such," Cat replied. He jumped off the wall and kicked Cat off the walkway. She caught the railing and pulled herself up. This time Mercy kneed Cat in her face knocking her to the lower levels of the ship's divide. "You don't look like my equal from down there!" Mercy taunted. She killed two marauders before she took cover from the dual magnums. "C'mon Cat I expected better from you." "You asked for it," she mumbled in her helmet. Cat popped out of cover and launched an energy wave at the master gunslinger. Mercy cursed in an ancient language and barely dodged the attack. Shots rained down as Mercy pulled himself up.

Marauders covered their leader as he stood to his feet. "What are your orders sir?" one asked. "Fall back to the hangars we need to get out of here." Cat watched as the NGO platoons and their leader retreated. "We can't let them escape." "Yes ma'am," a soldier responded. Cat jumped to the level above and pursued her target. The enemy fired on the scythe-wielder in an attempt to slow her down. One of them got lucky and landed a shot on her shoulder. It slowed her down but it didn't stop her. That's all Mercy needed to escape. He shut the doors that led to the hanger and then shot the controls. "Into the dropships now," he ordered. Mercy and his men boarded the transports and prepped for takeoff. Cat tried to override the door controls but figured they were destroyed. "Stand back," she said. The knights gave her some space as she launched another energy wave. It was already too late. The last of the dropships were already out of the hangar and in the air. Cat shook her head in disappointment, "Send out a seeker drone." The knight nodded and relayed the order. "Time to deal with Lazarus," she thought. The ship was stripped and searched for anything that would prove to be useful information. Cat left the ship with her scythe deactivated and resting on her back. She reported back to Lazarus and updated him on the current situation. Lazarus regained some of his strength and now towered over Cat. "How did he escape?" "A lucky shot and a sealed door," Cat responded. "Well why didn't you fly after him Cat?" The commander couldn't believe the question. "I can't fly like you Lazarus, duh." "Well you better learn kitty because I don't want him escaping. "I'll handle it Lazarus." "It should've been handled. Now Mercy is gone and you have no idea where he is." Her gauntlet beeped as a holo-map popped up, "I do now." "What do you plan to do Cat?" "I'm rolling in there with a heavy armor division and slaughtering Mercy and his men. I just ordered them to mobilize." Lazarus nodded, "Well get to it commander." She saluted her king before exiting the tent. The convoy of tanks and A.P.C.'s were moving through the isolation zone before heading out into the open land ahead. Cat casually walked as she hopped onto a tank. The elite commander waved her armored division forward with an esteemed look on her flawless face. She was about to bring the pain!

The drones pinpointed Mercy's location deep in the forest. It expanded for miles and provided plenty of advantages. The soldiers had to mind the bump as they traveled down the dirt road. They were tough as nails so the soldiers shouldn't mind much. The path was surrounded by massive trees that were hundreds of feet tall; foreboding trees that didn't let a lot of light in.

The coordinates for Mercy were still a few more clicks farther into the forest. Cat didn't like it one bit as she sat in the hue of the red light. An ominous feeling came over her as the convoy came to a halt. Cat stood up to open the hatch and popped out to see what was going on. Two knights exited the A.P.C. in front of her to examine the problem. "Why did we stop?" asked Cat. "There are up-rooted trees blocking our path. Attempting to remove them now," said the knight. "No! Don't remove the trees do you understand?" There was no response which meant they didn't hear her, or worse. Cat hopped down to the road and moved to the front of the convoy. The trees rustled causing leaves to fall to the ground. Her scythe activated on mental command alone as she waited. Mercy, as Cat expected, was high in the trees with his marauders waiting to strike. He raised his hand slowly signaling for his men to prepare and fire. The rocket launchers were mounted on their shoulders and they waited for the command.

He watched Cat to see how long it would be before she dropped her guard. She slowly eased out of her battle stance and lowered her infamous scythe. Mercy smirked at the opportunity and swiftly dropped his hand. Rockets rained down like due judgment from a malicious foe. The ground trembled underneath her boots as rockets struck near or on their desired target. Some A.P.C.'s and tanks were hit directly while others were brushed by the impact. Knight soldiers piled out and laid down suppressive fire while the tanks fired into the trees. "Don't forget about her," Mercy said. One of his men nodded and aimed down his sights. A squeeze of the trigger and the rocket was away. Cat recognized the incoming threat and tightened her grip on the haft of the scythe. Without a second thought she jumped to meet the rocket head on. The flat side of the scythe's blade smacked the rocket back to where it came from. Mercy quickly jumped from the tree to avoid the rocket strike. The blast shredded through the tree and anything in its path. The master sharpshooter pulled himself up from another narrow escape. "It's time to die kitty cat." He activated a weapon enhancement that allowed him to deal greater damage to his adversaries. An enhancement Mercy saved only for the toughest of opponents. Cat should consider herself honored since that enhancement was rarely used. Precision shots hammered down on Cat. The lucky shot Mercy had landed from earlier picked its worst time to take its toll on Cat. Her reflexes would've been more than enough to deflect the bolts. The problem was more physical than it was mental and it would only get worse.

One shot slipped pass, then another, then another, and another, and another, until a final shot was landed in the middle of her chest. The force of the shot knocked Cat to the ground. She finally realized that they were in deep trouble and all it took was a chest full of bolts. "Fall back!" she yelled as she scrambled to her feet. The remaining knights boarded the armored vehicles that were still operational and retreated back down the road. Mercy holstered his magnums and relished in victory. Cat hopped on a tank and slid down the hatch and closed it. She winced in pain as she felt the blast marks on her armor. "Are you alright commander?" the gunner asked. "I'm fine soldier just watch for any more hostiles." He nodded and turned back to his gun. A crushing defeat on her behalf and a blow to her ego. She had a reputation for mercilessly demolishing her enemy but instead she was bested. "Time to deal with Lazarus," Cat said.

An ugly streak of lightning arched through the roof of Lazarus' tent. "Are you mad?" she asked sarcastically. "I shouldn't be mad but I am." A puzzled look came over her tired face. "I knew your plan against Mercy wouldn't work. He's a weapons master for one. That means he knows all weapons and firearms inside and out. If it's a new weapon he'll take five minutes' tops to learn how to use it. Secondly he's a master in numerous warfare tactics." Cat folded her arms, "And I'm not?" Lazarus could tell she was offended by his comment. "You do know many tactics and strategies but you tend to stick with two." "What is that?" she asked. "Strength in numbers and heavy armor." "It never failed before!" she shouted. Cat rose her voice and Lazarus could feel the frustration in her comment. "But it did! Now Mercy is still alive and my knights dead." His red eyes started to burn hotter as the argument continued. "Why do you care anyway?! The standard knight comes cheap since they're all clones." Cat walked a few feet away from the desk trying to hold back her anger. "I care because they were wasted by a foolish girl playing commander." Lazarus didn't yell at her that time. His voice was low and cold and that comment pierced Cat deeper than the eye could see.

The blood in her veins boiled over throwing Cat into a rage. She threw the desk into the wall causing the room to shake. The royal guards outside of the tent looked at each other before they returned to their duties. Loud grunting and shouting sounded from the tent as did more shaking. The guards casually slid away until they were gone completely. Lazarus pinned her down with little effort. "All that energy you're wasting now could be directed at Mercy," he told her. "How am I supposed to pin Mercy down when he has an entire forest as his stomping ground?"

Lazarus tapped her on the head, "Use your brain." He removed himself and pulled Cat to her feet. She stood motionless pondering for a moment until the light bulb shined. "I got it!" she exclaimed while snapping her fingers. The plan she formulated was bold and had a smoldering end. "It's about time," he said harshly. Cat pulled a fast one and punched Lazarus straight into a wall. "That's my girl," he said lying on the floor. Cat ordered a squad of four specialized knights to be flown in to help. Once they were on the ground they were loaded into an A.P.C. and placed in the convoy. "It's time to finish this." Cat's armored division was in the forest once more. It seemed like the same plan as before but the only difference this time would be the outcome! Knights under her command were skeptical and were sure that they were all dead. Cat was aware of the skepticism and that's why she believed it would work, it had to work. Or else she would have to deal with Lazarus again. She certainly didn't want that.

The convoy came to a stop like before and knights attempted to remove the debris just like before. Mercy almost busted out in laughter and nearly gave up their position. "I considered her to be a smart one but I guess I was wrong about her. Oh well, fire!" Cat sprung from the tank and whipped energy waves from her scythe. The waves were blindly fired just to buy her convoy some time. "Everybody out of the vehicles now!" The knights piled out and started to fire into the branches above. Plasma bolts, a form of super-heated gas, ripped through the foliage and hit a few NGO marauders. Mercy knew that the knights were just blind-firing as well. "They can't see us, hurry up and fire," Mercy ordered. The marauders came to their senses and fired. The knights were on their feet this time and reacted quickly. Some were able to dodge the rockets while others weren't as lucky. The tanks blasted plasma rods, heavy rods that contained explosive plasma energy, after plasma rods into the forest hitting what they could. One rocket streaked towards the A.P.C. that contained the specialized knights. Another rocket streaked towards Cat herself. A high-powered shot from Mercy slowed her so what could a rocket do? She launched another energy wave wielding her scythe back-handed this time. The rocket was destroyed and the A.P.C. was saved but the same couldn't be said for Cat. The impact of the rocket sent the commander through the forest, toppling a few trees. The A.P.C. opened its doors and the surprise gift came out to play. They were Incinerator Knights that carried lethal flamethrowers. Mercy's eyes widen behind his helmet. WHOOSH! Flames spewed from the nozzle of the flamethrowers. The unique weapon was built in a way that the use of canisters were obsolete.

All of the design specifications were quite advanced on how a such a thing could be possible. The things that they needed to know was that the flames emitted were capable of reducing a man to ashes and that they could shoot over six hundred yards. Some marauders were caught in the blue flames while other barely dodged them. "Whoa that's hot!" Mercy was right, the sheer heat that radiated from the flamethrowers could set something on fire. He didn't wait around to witness such a thing. Mercy was fast but he couldn't out run the fire. Cat removed a tree trunk that laid on top of her, "Status." "We have him on the run ma'am," one flame-spitter said. "Good, take to the sky and keep it that way." "Yes ma'am." They activated their jetpacks and went airborne. Her legs were removed from beneath a few more tree trunks and she then leaped into the blazing inferno. Cat landed on the branch like she was the lightest of feathers. Mercy balanced on a branch that was only a single bound from her. "Well, well, if it isn't my favorite kitty. Burn!" A barrage of laser bolts zipped pass Cat's head. The commander swung around to the back and used the tree as cover. The laser bolts hissed as they impacted the tree. A swift chop cut the top half of the tree allowing Cat to kick it towards Mercy. He quickly dodged the incoming debris and hopped to another tree. They chased after one another like they played a game of leap-frog. Only difference was that if one landed on the other it would be fatal.

The flames licked the trunk of a tree not far from their position. Cat landed dangerously close to Mercy and unleashed an energy wave. The sharpshooter bent all the way backwards until his body was parallel to the branch. He reacted by sweeping Cat off her feet and blasting her at point blank range. It was astounding that the commander was able to deflect every last one of the bolts. Mercy cursed as he jumped from the branch to another tree. Little did he know that the tree was about to give-way. Mercy was shocked to see that the tree was gone and he slammed face first into another tree. The deadly marksman tumbled from one branch to the next without the chance to catch himself. He crashed in a small clearing with branches all over him. The suppressed thud noted the arrival of his adversary. "Do I look like your equal now?" Mercy aimed his wrist bracer, "Never!" He fired an explosive flechette that Cat barely dodged and that gave Mercy enough time to take the offensive. A flechette is a type of small ammunition that was in the form of a small dart. Mercy customized his own flechette's to explode on contact. As soon as she landed she was bombarded by laser bolts. An endless stream of bolts were spewed from the infamous dual magnums. "I was born to kill peasants like you!" Mercy shouted. "Fool I'm one of a kind," Cat responded.

The spinning cyclone of a scythe deflected every bolt as she closed in. Mercy's back was against the flames as he continued to shoot. He ran out of room and out of time. The plasma-edged blade of her scythe sliced clean through one of his magnums. No one was ever that close to Mercy unless he allowed it. This is the moment he knew he had met his match. Cat dashed forward and stopped right in front of Mercy meeting him eye-to-eye. She dodged the shot and flip-kicked him to the ground. He laid on the ground thinking it was impossible for him to be challenged by anyone. "What's the matter? Cat got your tongue?" Mercy pulled his knife and prepared to attack, "Hardly." An odd sensation originated from his back all the way to his chest. A scarring sensation that had nothing to do with fire but . . . plasma! "End-game Mercy." Cat ripped the scythe from his back and in one clean stroke, took off his head. She caught his head and watched as his lifeless body fell to the ground. A befitting end for a man who didn't see his opponent as his equal.

The familiar rush of air rustled his hair as he sat behind the desk. Her violet armor was blackened and scorched by the flames of the forest fire. A scorched helmet that belonged to the former sharpshooter was placed on his desk. Lazarus picked up the helmet and looked inside to see if Mercy's head was still there. "Impressive Cat. This was a nice touch too," he said referring to the decapitated head. "He deserved it. He shot his mouth off way too much." Lazarus stood to reveal his refurbished armor and new crimson cape. "You did well Cat but next time try not to burn down my entire forest." "No promises," she replied. Lazarus strode towards the door with Cat on his arm. "That was the last of his lieutenants and now Onyx is vulnerable. When do we strike?" she asked. Onyx was the leader of the New Galactic Order. Lazarus final task was to deal with Onyx. "Soon commander. My only question for you is what will you do when you see her?" Cat knew exactly what he was talking about. "I'll do my job." Lazarus eyed Cat for a moment. "Very well, let's get to it."

Malevolent End

Another blast rocked *Oblivion's Edge* as they orbited the planet of Earth. The anti-spacecraft cannons, or ASC, were unloading everything they had on the Chevalier Star Fleet. Onyx made an effective defensive system against Lazarus. He couldn't enter the atmosphere until the cannons were destroyed. That's why Lazarus was sending his best to deal with that problem. A massive ground assault would be inserted via dropships and knight forces will assault the cannons head on. They will be the distraction for the three specialized teams who will flank the cannons and proceed to destroy them. After that problem is solved designated frigates would insert reinforcements and the final assault would begin. Cat looked over the plan one last time as she prepped for insertion. The holo-map dissipated back into her gauntlet as she entered the dropship. There waiting for her was a four man team of highly trained knight commandos. They were the best of the best and they're the ones that deal with the most important objectives.

The knight commandos always got the job done even if it took the dying breath from the last man to accomplish it. Their armor was optimized greatly from the normal suit due to the extreme need for combat efficiency. "Ready for some combat boys?" Cat asked. "Always Commander. This is DELTA team and I'm team lead Hunter." The Firstborn and commando shook hands. "That's Vaxer, Titan, and Talon," he said pointing at the others. They were all stern knights ready to do what's necessary. "We'll be fighting beside you every step of the way Commander," Hunter promised. "That's what I like to hear," replied Cat. The doors on the dropship closed and a red light covered the knights. The dropship was lifted off the ground and was hoisted over open space. Thousands of other dropships were suspended just like theirs and waited to be dropped. Cat was one of the most hardened warriors in the universe but she hated orbital drops. "You alright Commander?" Vaxer asked. Cat nodded, "I'm fine I just simply hate what comes next." The signal was given and one by one the dropships were released into outer space below. Initially when they drop there is this momentary sensation of weightlessness that causes everyone to rise out of their seats. Once the pilots activate the thrusters everyone is jammed back into their seats and the ride begins. Cat stood firmly in the cockpit with the pilots and observed their descent into combat hell. Cannon fire exploded right and left.

It was a great deal of skill and a bit of luck that they were still alive. The pilots saw something that even Cat couldn't see. That's why they were the ones flying the dropship. They weaved here and there and barrel-rolled to avoid the incoming cannon fire. A dropship next to theirs was hit and spiraled out of control before exploding. 18 men were lost in one transport. War was a deadly game that would take everybody's life sooner or later. Cat knew it was inevitable but she was gonna postpone that fate until her job was done. The colossal orbital insertion started breaking through the atmosphere of Earth. Hunter tapped Titan on his shoulder and passed him a grenade. They passed through the clouds that caused a little bit of turbulence before the ground was actually visible. The ASC cannons could be seen blasting away into the sky. "There they are," Cat said to herself. Humid air started to fill the passenger cabin and cockpit as they descended to the battlefield. The pilots leveled out the dropship and continued to evade hostile cannon fire. "I'll see you guys back home," the pilot said before breaking off. The pilots skillfully swooped low into the city streets and used the surrounding structures as cover.

The doors on the dropship opened as Cat

moved out of the cockpit. The dropship sped through the tight paths in between the structures. Cat grabbed on to a handle so she could lean out a bit. The enemy lurked in the vacant building that was before the speeding dropship. A squad of NGO soldiers heard the sounds of thruster engines and spotted the dropship. One man stood, mounted the rocket launcher over his shoulder and fired. The rocket came so fast that the pilots barely had time to react. The pilots did what they could but they couldn't avoid the rocket. It struck near the rear-end of the dropship and knocked them out of the sky. The dropship slammed into a building before it crashed and slid to a smoking halt. Smoke and dust filled the passenger cabin making it hard to see. Circuits sparked and sizzled as Cat sat up. She rubbed her head as she looked around for her scythe. It was a good thing that Zeno optimized her scythe for compact mode. It made it easier for her to carry the scythe around. She placed it on her back and kneeled as the others came too. They grabbed their plasma rifles and checked their equipment. "Our pilots are dead," Talon informed the rest. Hunter nodded as he peered out into the buildings above. "I don't see anything yet," Hunter said. "Yeah, me neither. Let's get out of this thing before they fire another rocket," Cat cautioned. Hunter agreed and gestured for his men to move out. Titan was the first one out and secured the perimeter as the others got out.

As soon as all of them were out laser bolts started to fly. The laser bolts zipped pass their heads as they burrowed themselves into their cover. The commandos popped out and started firing at all known hostile positions. One laser bolt nailed Talon in his shoulder causing him to jerk back. Cat deflected a few bolts before checking on Talon. "You alright?" Talon nodded in response. "You good killer?" Hunter asked while firing. "I'm fine just really ticked off." Talon rose up and unloaded a barrage plasma bolts on the enemy. He dropped back down to vent his rifle. Reloading was a thing of the past with their plasma rifles. They just had to vent every now and then when the rifle's core overheated. Whenever they vented their rifles the commandos were just releasing all the steam. Vaxer activated his goggles and scanned the buildings that surrounded them. Hostile heat signatures blazed hot white all around them. Vaxer pointed to all marked enemy positions for Hunter to see. The team lead looked around before giving him the green light. "Light 'em up Vax!" The commando dropped his rifle and armed his Magnetic Plasma Launcher. The MPL fired blistering rods of plasma that exploded on contact. The commando zeroed in on the position and fired the MPL. The rod blasted from the launcher and hit the target. That portion of the building exploded with a blue static haze. He blasted away at one position after another with pinpoint accuracy. Anyone caught in the blast was completely charred. The laser bolts ceased to rain down and the streets grew quiet. The only sounds that filled the air constantly was from the distant battle.

Vaxer scanned the positions once more to make sure all threats were dead. "All clear." Cat moved from behind the crashed dropship as she deactivated her scythe. She checked the map to see their current position. "The ASC cannon is two clicks from here boys, let's get to humping," Cat told them. "You heard the lady," Hunter started, "Let's get moving." They moved through the streets smoothly and swiftly. They checked their corners, watched their blind spots, and always scanned the rooftops. They watched each other's backs as they moved through the hostile territory. The sun's blistering rays weighed down on the Firstborn and commandos. They walked down a tight alleyway that was cluttered with trash and other content. Titan lowered his rifle as he felt something originating in his feet. "You guys feel that?" Titan asked. "Yeah I feel it too," Vaxer replied. It was a rumbling sensation that continued grow as they neared the exit of the alley. Out of the blue came an enemy tank rolling pass the alley. "Drop," Hunter alerted. The entire team moved into cover and hid from the tank. It rolled pass unaware of what lurked in the alley. Hunter peaked his head out and gave the all-clear.

The team stood up once more and made their way to the exit. Suddenly the tank rolled back in front of the exit and aimed at the knights. Hunter and his men dropped to the ground to evade the shot. Cat could feel the pure force that followed the shot. The Firstborn grabbed the tank, threw it in the air, and sliced it apart. The halves of the tank crash back down with a loud thud. The commandos stared in disbelief for a moment. They never saw a Firstborn display their power up close before. It was a shocking experience even for them. Talon walked over to the tank and took a good look at it. "How come Firstborns weren't mass produced like us?" "Because our power is one of kind Talon." He nodded as he moved on. "Let's keep moving we're almost there," said Hunter.

Half a click later they arrived at the cannon and prepared to neutralize all threats. The cannon rested on top of this large tower that housed unknown components so the cannon could work. The objective was to take out the control room. "Eyes on the prize gentlemen," Cat told them. "Arm grapnel hooks," Hunter ordered. Grapnel hooks was a device that allowed quick transversal to the rooftops or other tall structures. All men armed their grapnel hooks and aimed for the railing far above. The grapnel hooks were launched into the heights above and secured themselves. One after another they were whisked away towards the top. The humid air rushed pass them as they climbed the side of the cannon's tower. They stylishly landed on the platform and engaged the NGO soldiers. The human soldiers were no match for the elite commandos. They picked their targets off with precision shots. Cat slid across the ground tripping a few before slashing all of them with her scythe. She dodged a laser bolt before planting her scythe into the man's chest. Cat slapped another soldier's rifle away before tossing him over the edge of the tower. "That's all of them for now," Vaxer said. They moved over to a service hatch that led into the tower. "Get down there and plant those charges knights," ordered Cat.

Laser bolts zipped pass noting the arrival of more NGO soldiers. Cat deflected a few bolts, "Go I got this." The commandos pried open the hatch and proceeded down into the tower. They moved through the dark hallways towards the control center. "You sure she's fine up there by herself?" Titan asked. Hunter turned to his comrade, "You saw what she did to the tank right?" Titan nodded in remembrance. "She's fine trust me. Let's just take this place offline," Hunter told them. The team reached the door that led to the control center. They could hear the operators on the inside. They were still buzzing about rapidly working to destroy the Chevalier Star Fleet. Hunter signaled for Talon to step up.

The commando placed a charge on the door and stood back. Talon gripped the detonator, "I love when things go boom." He hit the button and the door was shredded open. The ones closest to the door were killed from the blast while others were knocked to the ground. The lethal knights rushed like they practiced so many times before and executed all threats. Vaxer rammed one operator to the ground and fired plasma bolts into the operator's chest. Hunter picked two others off with accurate head-shots. One operator hid behind his console while the others were being slaughtered. He popped up quickly and aimed for the commandos' leader. Titan seized the enemy operator's hand and littered his body with plasma bolts. The blistering bolts ripped through his body with ease. "I owe you one Titan," Hunter said. The Delta Team commandos started placing charges all over the center. "All charges are set boss," Vaxer informed. "Alright let's get out of here," Hunter ordered. They moved out into the hallway to receive more enemy fire. "Whoa!" they shouted before dropping down. "Cover fire! Cover FIRE!" Hunter commanded. Vaxer and Talon rose to a knee and suppressed the enemy so the other two could retreat. Laser bolts sizzled pass their helmets as they unflinchingly continued to fire. The commandos are nothing to trifle with. "Hunter this is the Commander. The platform is secured once more and the dropship is here for exfiltration." Hunter dodged a bolt before responding. "Understood Commander on our way. We gotta get topside for dust-off, move!"

Vaxer and Talon stood to their feet and backed their way down the hall while firing. The team reached the ladder that led to the service and one by one they climbed. Titan tossed a few grenades to cover their escape. They reached the surface of the platform and saw the dropship waiting for them. Hunter stood next to the dropship while the others piled in. The team leader sat down on the floor and fired at the NGO soldiers exiting the service hatch. A sudden plasma rod streaked out of nowhere and blew the service hatch closed. Hunter looked over his shoulder to see Vaxer wielding the smoking MPL. "I got your back Hunter." Their leader grinned at the comment as he acquired a seat. "Good work knights, real good work," Cat praised. Talon nudged Titan and started a countdown. They all watched as he hit zero and witnessed the explosion. The control center was obliterated, taking the cannon offline. "I love explosions," said Talon. The other cannons were taken offline and the fleet was safe. "All cannons are offline Lazarus. You can send in the reinforcements now," Cat informed the King. "Acknowledged Commander sending them in now. Get ready to have some sand in your boots knights," Lazarus told them.

Cat's hologram nodded before it deactivated. Lazarus turned his attention to the frigates that descended to Earth. It was the beginning of the end for Onyx and it only grew closer. A malevolent end in a matter of fact. Admiral Turrok stood next to his King as *Oblivion's Edge* started its descent as well. Lazarus tightened his fists, "Time to cut the head off of the snake."

****

The skies were filled with chaos. Star ships and star cruisers destroyed one another. *Oblivion's Edge* held its own against three NGO star cruisers. Lazarus' flag ship made quick work of the enemy cruisers. The Y-winged Falcon star fighters darted back and forth in intense savage dog fights. You could tell who were the more experienced pilots just by the maneuvers. It was an incredible sight to witness. On the ground was a battle of an equal magnitude waged as well. Main Battle Tanks, Gunships, A.P.C.'s, and knight soldiers took on the NGO forces. It was one of the most destructive battles if not the most destructive battle to date. This war was literally hell on Earth. The entire country of New

Egypt was a raging inferno. Anyone who was never use to war would feel overwhelmed and petrified due to the sheer scale of the battles. Lazarus wasn't effected at all. In fact, he was focusing on his own upcoming battle. The magnificent palace was constructed near the pyramids that were only a few miles away.

Lazarus floated inches above the ground as he crossed the bridge that led to the palace. Pillars stood on both sides of the vast bridge that had Egyptian hieroglyphs on every last one of them. He noticed one hieroglyph that depicted Onyx. The massive doors parted and granted entry to the guest. Inside the palace was a very long hallway that stretched into darkness. Lazarus looked up to see no ceiling in sight just mist and more darkness. Pools of fire erupted to light the path. More hieroglyphs covered the walls from end to end. One depiction was when the Firstborn initially invaded Earth and unleashed their godly power. Another depiction showed Onyx being worshiped. The humans were treating Onyx as their deity, their God. Humans are such lost creatures, always searching for something or someone to follow. When they can't find one they'll create one. It was best that someone did lead them. They are a young race but destructive and reckless. So in truth the human-race will always need someone or something to lead them. Lazarus didn't care for being worshiped, he just wanted to reign. His desire to rule is what sparked the feud between the Firstborns. Now he seemed to end it all here and now.

Massive doors parted once more, this time, to reveal the throne room. Large marble statues of Onyx lined the throne room on both sides. The real Onyx sat on the throne. His appearance had changed greatly since the last time Lazarus saw him. Onyx sat on the throne like he was the exalted Ramses The Great. "Onyx, I will offer you this chance once and only once. Kneel before me and I will grant you mercy." Onyx looked his younger brother over before he stood. "How dare you come to my kingdom, my planet, my throne, and demand ME to kneel?" Onyx' golden eyes flashed purple for a moment as he stared at his brother. He exploded from the throne and rammed shoulder-first into Lazarus. The young Firstborn smashed through a statue causing the marble colossus to topple. "I'm not here to talk," Onyx said. "Thank the Architects. This would've been much more boring." Lazarus hopped over the fallen statue and engaged Onyx in hand-to-hand combat. Onyx fighting style was an animalistic ground-and-pound. He utilized the 'power blow' energy technique a lot more then Lazarus did. A 'power blow' was a basic move like a punch or a kick but was amplified by their bio-energy. Lazarus' style was a much more slick and polished fighting style. He would pull clever feigns and other deceptive maneuvers like his shading ability during one-on-one combat. Lazarus attempted to fire an energy blast but Onyx slapped his hand away causing another statue to topple. Onyx caught the statue and threw it at his brother. Lazarus counter-threw the statue back only for it to be destroyed with one punch. Onyx dashed forward and delivered three power blows that juggled Lazarus' organs.

The young Firstborn stumbled backwards falling to one knee. Onyx must've been training since the last time they had seen each other. Lazarus was lifted off the ground by his throat. "You can't hope to beat me? After all you are my little brother," Onyx told him. "C'mon Onyx you know that never stopped me before." The Firstborn pharaoh nodded quietly in agreement. "What about death? Has death ever stopped you Lazarus?" Lazarus' expression changed behind his helmet. "Well of course not Onyx I've never died before so . . . oh I see where you're going with this." Onyx's face mask activated, "Well let's see." Onyx raised Lazarus high above his head before bringing him down full force on his knee and then threw him. Lazarus crashed through a number of walls before finally exploding from the palace. He skipped across the dessert ground before coming to a halt. A loud crack of thunder signified that Onyx had taken to the sky but when Lazarus looked up Onyx was walking towards him.

"Once I kill you here on Earth I will return to Chevalier and drag your corpse through the city streets and show the people what I did to their marvelous king. That's if I don't completely vaporize you!" Onyx blasted Lazarus back a few more feet. Lazarus rolled over to his feet and faced Onyx. "You have to catch me first."

****

Cat sliced and diced through her enemies like

soggy bread. It wasn't even a challenge for the Firstborn. Cat was sinister with her scythe in combat. She trained with Lazarus before all the madness and chaos. A good thing she did learn and perfect her skills. With a single swing she killed three NGO soldiers and kicked another into a building. A dropship streaked overhead and deployed Two berserkers. The gigantic brutes armed their gravity hammers and attacked knight soldiers. The hammers sent soldiers flying in every direction. With one strike a berserker destroyed a tank. Those brutes were about to meet their match. "My turn to deal some pain." Cat sprinted across the battlefield and stayed low like a wolf. She flipped her scythe upside down while she was sprinting and threw it. The scythe ripped through the air and slammed into one berserker. The berserker fell back in pain, leaving the other to deal with Cat one-on-one. The Commander directed the first swing away and evaded the second one. The berserker was big and slow and Cat was far too nimble. She broke one of his legs, punched him in his stomach, and tore the hammer from his clutches. "Let's see how you like it," she said. Cat dropped the hammer on the beast's head killing it. One down, one to go. The last berserker recovered from the wound and attacked the Firstborn. Cat blocked the hammer strike that destroyed her weapon as well as knocked her back. "They pack a mean punch. I better make this quick," she said to herself. Cat dodged a second hammer swing, reclaimed her scythe and then decapitated the brute.

The massive pile of enhanced muscle fell to the hot desert ground. "I thought berserkers were tough," she said twirling her scythe. The Commander was about to jump back into the fray before she sensed something. A great energy level she hasn't felt in a long time. It was coming up on her backside and she had to do something fast. But it was too late. A tremendous force rocked Cat off her feet and sent her flying. The Firstborn soared through the air before slicing through a star fighter, completely destroying it. She then crashed through a few buildings before coming to a halt. The city streets were filled with chaos just like in front of the pyramids.

An enemy tank spotted the Commander and rammed her against a building. The tank operators didn't know of the Firstborn's profound strength. Cat tossed the tank into the air and then split it in half. The wreckage slammed back onto the ground. Another Firstborn landed on the street behind Cat. "Not bad, not bad at all. You could've done better though." Cat turned to face her new threat. "Better than you Flare?" Flare paced to her right before answering. "No but you could have done better." Cat rolled her eyes at the predictable response. "Maybe I will next time," responded Cat. "There won't be a next time." The Commander was able to block the attack that time. She felt the same tremendous force that sent her flying earlier. "You just might live long enough to see us win this war," Flare said. The Firstborns activated their helmets and armed their weapons. The duel between the two was a rugged one. It was hit-for-hit and block-for-block in their battle. Flare's shotos moved at blinding speeds due to the skill of the master. Cat swung on Flare who dodged the strike. Her scythe jammed into the piece of tank she destroyed previously. "Oh this is just perfect," she complained. Cat deflected two strikes and then threw Flare into the wreckage causing her to roll backwards. Flare frowned behind her helmet before she took action. Flare grabbed the other piece of the tank and picked it up, "Catch!" Cat retrieved her scythe, evaded the debris and flung the wreckage. Flare jumped towards the debris, sliced through it and knocked Cat back. The High Priestess then hurled the Commander into the air. Cat crashed onto a roof and was closely followed by Flare. "C'mon Cat really try to impress me." "Oh I will," Cat said before lashing out.

****

Onyx and Lazarus chased one another through the burning skies. They flew faster than any other star fighter in the skies. The red eyed Firstborn barrel-rolled to the left to dodge debris. Onyx smashed through and continued to pursue his brother. They zipped left, right, up, down, and diagonal all across the vast sky. The two of them flew in close to one of the cruisers during their chase. Onyx fired his Death Stare, they were golden energy beams that originated from his eyes. Lazarus easily evaded the first barrage and continued to fly. "Surely you can do better Onyx!" Onyx fired again, this time in front of his intended target. The explosion knocked the young Firstborn out of his flight path. Lazarus recovered quickly using a stationary turret and kicked Onyx into the star cruiser. The brute of a man broke through wall after wall inside the ship. He came to a sliding stop in the mess hall.

Onyx dodged the homing attack from his opponent and then broke a table on top of Lazarus. "Did you ever wonder what the after-life holds for you?" Onyx asked. "You're insane if you think I'm going to die," Lazarus shot back. Onyx parried the punch but received a firm kick to the face. Lazarus followed up with a savage palm-strike to Onyx' spine and then body-slammed his older brother. Onyx was quick in seizing Lazarus' hands and crushing his wrists. "I grow tired of this foolish game," Onyx told him. "Well let me heat it up." Lazarus broke free from the grasp of death and fired two energy beams into Onyx' chest. The Firstborn was blasted from the cruiser and was launched into orbit. The Supreme Overlord sliced through the engines of a star cruiser causing it to malfunction. Onyx floated there in space for a moment before Lazarus came for his head. The King delivered a stomach crushing knee to Onyx and then a strong slap. Onyx flipped around and fired energy blast after energy blast at overwhelming speeds. Lazarus quickly shaded the volley and executed a nine-piece combo of power blows that rocked his opponent. The young Firstborn was locked in and focused on his target now. That meant Onyx was in trouble. The Overlord seized Lazarus' arm and landed a devastating left hook. The blow was so powerful that Lazarus' entire helmet shattered into pieces. "How'd that taste," growled Onyx. "It tasted like this." Lazarus head-butted Onyx and then placed him in a chokehold. "Let's see if this kills you," Lazarus said. They plummeted towards the Earth faster than a meteor. It would all be over soon.

****

Cat and Flare continued their fight among the chaos. Cat unleashed energy waves through her scythe. The energy waves demolished entire buildings and anyone caught in its path. Her scythe twirled smoothly on her hands. The building toppled over and smashed into other buildings. The shattered glass from the skyscrapers sprinkled the Firstborn as they fought. Cat scored three blows on Flare's helmet, enraging her. Flare utilized her Mammoth Charge and tackled Cat through an entire parking garage. Flare's Mammoth Charge was a powerful ramming attack she used to knock her opponents back. Her Mammoth charge could demolish entire buildings. The Commander skidded across tattered asphalt and debris as the multilevel garage fell. "Just die!" Flare shouted as she drove her little sister into the ground. "Never," Cat responded. Cat gained the upper hand, threw Flare into the air and then jumped up to launch Flare back into the rubble. Cat then levitated in place as she unleashed a flurry of energy waves. Dust and rubble flew everywhere as the onslaught continued. Soldiers were blown away along with their vehicles.

With every impact Flare was driven further and further into the ground. The High Priestess couldn't even think to block the attack because of how powerful it was. Bioelectricity started to surge and spark off of Cat's body as her energy continued to build. The energy waves slowly started to die down before they stopped altogether. The dust began to settle as Cat landed and walked over to where her opponent laid. Flare's armor was destroyed and the eye slits on her helmet were cracked. "You should have never tried me Flare. This is what happens when you push me." Cat scanned over Flare's decommissioned body. They deactivated their helmets so they could talk face to face. Flare started laughing as blood dripped from her lips. "You say it like you could've killed me Cat. We both know you would never kill me." Flare's hand crept closer and closer to her shoto that was in reach. "You're right Flare. The fact that we're sisters is pretty much the only reason why you're alive right now. Remember that." Flare frowned, "remember this!" Flare grabbed her shoto and lashed out in one last powerful slash. Cat reacted quickly by flipping upwards dodging the attack and crashed back down knees first. The impact knocked Flare unconscious on top of the rubble. Cat kneeled over her sister feeling some remorse. She wished they were never enemies. Suddenly, a loud blast of thunder disrupted everything. Everybody watched as the burning comet descend out the sky and crash. The impact caused a massive sand cloud to erupt. Cat deactivated her scythe and placed it on her back. She moved quick in order to reach the pyramids. Cat had to make sure that Lazarus was still alive. Lazarus and Onyx were in a power lock with raw energy surging throughout their bodies. The output of their combined power caused the entire planet to shake. A spectacle like this was rarely ever seen. "You cannot match my power Lazarus." Onyx pulled a fast one and stunned his opponent. Lazarus staggered back before the Overlord wrapped his hands around his throat. Lazarus was lifted off of the ground, "I will reduce you to ashes!" Onyx activated his Death Stare to finish his adversary. Lazarus saw this as his last chance to end it. He covered Onyx's eyes causing the beams to backfire and explode in his face. The flash of light blinded anyone who was observing. There was a momentary silence that hung in the air. A feeling of fear and uncertainty crept up on every living soul that was present. This moment defined the future of the entire universe. Out of the dust emerged two figures, one dragged the other. The Firstborn was tossed like common trash. "You're free now. You no longer have to fight as Onyx's slaves."

The soldiers threw down their weapons as Lazarus expected but then they did the unexpected. They lifted their leader off the ground and carried him back to his palace. Citizens who were hiding emerged and followed their wounded Overlord. Some even offered a helping hand. A long line of uncountable people snaked towards the palace. Lazarus floated towards the front of the line seeking his brother. Onyx gestured for them to stop. The helmet and Egyptian headdress he wore was blown from his head. Colors of gold and vibrant teal were faded from combat. "I don't understand," Lazarus uttered. "To you I am a tyrant but to them I am salvation." Onyx meant every word he had spoken and everyone else knew it too. The march continued and Lazarus was left in bewilderment. Cat gently pulled Lazarus back to reality. "C'mon let's get out of here," she said. All Chevalier Forces were rounded up on dropships. The wounded were placed on medivacs and were sent up first. Any equipment that was left behind was destroyed.

Onyx's forces headed to the palace to console their leader. Flare was retrieved as well and placed beside her Overlord in respect. Lazarus and Cat entered the bridge of *Oblivion's Edge* and walked towards the front. Turrok walked over to his king to ask about the outcome of the battle. "Sir what happened down there?" Lazarus stood motionless as he stared over the ruins of New Egypt. "It's over Admiral, the Power Struggle is finally over. Chart a course for home." Turrok nodded and relayed the orders. The star fleet ascended to space and prepared the jump to light speed. Lazarus didn't feel like a hero or a conqueror, not even a king. He just felt like a little boy who bested his older brother in a fist fight. Countless lives lost because of the simple act of greed. No sense of nobility nor honor in war. It only determines who's left in the end.

The White Rider

The others were finished with their assignments and have gone back to the realms they've made their homes. They ran into complications of course but they still got the job done. Now they got to rest and Archeus was the only who still had to finish his assignment. The Horseman entered the realm in search of the portal but something happened. He can't really remember what came afterward. His eyes were closed and out of consciousness but the ability to feel wasn't suppressed. The body could still feel the sensation of something warm and moist dripping over his skin. A very unpleasant, creamy feeling that encompassed his entire body up to his neck. Anybody who was in this position would be horrified or filled with terror for they knew that their time has come to an end.

Archeus finally came through the thick barrier of unconsciousness and found himself hanging upside down. The rider was wrapped and strung up in a thick cocoon made out of something in between spit, slime, and other bodily fluids. It smelled completely repulsing. Flies wouldn't even want to be around this crap. Slowly it started to come back to Archeus. He traveled into this realm and made his way towards the portal before he was attacked by these reptilian-like creatures. They had long talons and could switch in between walking on all fours or walking on two legs. They also had mandibles on both sides of their mouth that housed razor sharp rows of needle teeth. They swarmed around the rider and was able to get the better of him and drag him back to their twisted little hovel.

Archeus hung there for a moment as he thought of a way to escape. The reptiles stripped him of his weapons and equipment, even his wrist blades. Those freaks were very thorough when they searched him. He would cast a spell but the cocoon was one of magic as well that cancelled out his abilities. That's when he noticed the burning torch to the side of him. "Well it's better than nothing." He started swinging back and forth until the cocoon was over the torch a few times and caught fire. The cocoon was highly flammable and the entire thing went up in flames. Archeus winched at the pain a little bit as the cocoon began to weaken under the heat. The rider flexed his muscles and burst free from the disgusting trap and fell from the roof. Archeus landed on his feet as he met the cavern floor with a suppressed thud. He rose while throwing his hood onto his head, "Now I need to find my weapons."

The lair in which he was taken was a massive underground cavern that had an elaborate system of interconnecting tunnels and caves. If one didn't know his way around they would be lost until one of the reptilians caught them. Archeus followed the tracks on the ground to see where they would lead. He came up on a cave that was patrolled by a group of creatures. The three of them hissed at each other as they spoke in their natural language. Two of the reptiles started to walk out of the cave to check on the others. Once they were out of ear-shot the rider dropped down and approached very stealthily. The humanoid-like reptile was standing on two legs as he was completely unaware of the coming danger. Archeus wrapped his hands around the creature's mouth and neck while breaking his leg. He shouted but it was muffled by the rider's hand so the reptile couldn't alert the others. "Where are my weapons?" The reptile knew the Horseman meant business so he gave it up. "Your bow and other possessions are right inside there. You just have to get pass the others." He let out a chuckle before Archeus snapped his neck dropping the corpse to the ground. "Now that's funny." He stuck close to the wall as he crept into the room. The creatures wander talking with hisses and an annoying lisp. Archeus knelt behind some rocks as the reptiles noticed the body. "Our brother is down!" one shouted. The pack ran into the other room to check. Archeus moved to his weapons and armed himself. His dual wrist-blades were armed along with his dual short swords. Archeus grabbed his mystic bow **Nemesis** and the shadow quiver next. The bow had an 'Eye of Providence' on the front of it that helps the rider with aiming. He doesn't use it that often at all but when he does the symbol glows. It acts as a scope for him and extended his range to even greater distances. His shadow quiver is bottomless so that he has an unlimited amount of arrows. It took a great deal of magic and time but he finally got it done. **Nemesis** was a very powerful bow but the lizards won't be able to experience that.

One reptile turned, "the prisoner has escaped, kill him!" Archeus quick fired an arrow that greeted a reptile in his head. He smoothly transitioned from his bow to his short swords and cut another reptile to the ground. Archeus dodged a thrown lance and slashed two more of his enemies. Their screams echoed throughout the caves. The two short swords were placed in the reptile's scaly chest before they were retrieved by The White Rider as he kicked off. He sheathed his weapons as the rest of the nest became aware of the escaped prisoner. Archeus knew it wouldn't be long until they found him so he had to think of something quick. The rider started feeling and knocking on the wall for a hollow spot.

One such spot was discovered and from the feel of it that certain spot was much cooler. "There could be a water source on the other side of this wall," he said to himself. Archeus could hear the rough footsteps of more reptilians coming his way. He moved from the wall, "I'm not waiting to find out." He aimed his bow at the spot and fired an explosive arrow. The wall exploded into the next room revealing a very massive cavern. It was a water oasis like he guessed. This cavern housed a massive water reservoir that had several cascading falls and eventually somewhere else. "There he is!" a reptile shouted. Archeus wasted no time diving into the reservoir below. The rider swam underneath the water as lances shot through intended for him. The current swept him away and sent him tumbling down to the second pool of water. A lance passed over his shoulder and glanced across his cheek. Archeus spun around and quickly fired **Nemesis** killing another reptilian. "Too Close!" He fell to a third pool where the current was much swifter. More lances were thrown but smashed against the top of the tunnel entrance. Archeus was rushed towards the light at the end of the tunnel until he was met by fresh-clean air. The stream carried the Horseman over the edge into a steep cliff. Archeus slid across that before he flew over the canopy of the dense jungle. The moist air rushed pass the rider as he fell. His short swords were armed as he neared the massive trees. Archeus passed through the canopy and smashed a thick branch in two. He hit a few more branches before he dug his blades into a tree trunk. Bark was peeled from its home as Archeus slowed to a stop.

He opened his pale-silver eyes to see that he stopped inches above the ground. The rider looked up, "well that was fun." He rotated his shoulder since it was a little sore from the fall. He then pulled out his talisman to only find it fractured. The mystical item must have been broken during the fall. Either way he has to find the portal or else this would be a very short quest. Archeus never memorized the exact coordinates to the suspected location only a direction, east. The rider should've studied the directions like Death told him but of course he didn't listen. All he needed was the talisman and he would be fine. Too bad that way of thinking was terribly flawed.

The rider had to go on foot because the jungle paths were too congested with vegetation, roots that were the size of humanoid limbs, vines, and other natural material. Murrain, his trusty steed, wouldn't last that long in this realm. Not because she's weak but because she wouldn't stand for such a hot place. Archeus continued his hike through the jungle in his quest for the portal. He stopped every now and then to scout the path ahead before he kept moving through the jungle. The White Rider stood just above the canopy looking around trying to figure out the next step. As he stood there a flock of birds flew pass him because they were startled. That's when he noticed movement underneath the canopy. Archeus dipped underneath the thick leaves to see if he could spot anything. There was nothing he could spot at first but he sensed danger. His eyes became combat glazed while he continued to search, danger is very close by.

An arrow zipped pass his head as he flipped

to a branch beneath him. Whoever they are they missed, the arrow was meant for his head. The only thing that was worse than that was that Archeus didn't know where the shot came from. The archers had to be gilded by strong magic in order for a Horseman not to see them. A barrage of arrows was fired this time but Archeus dodged them easily. In retaliation he fired three arrows back at the same time in the general area where he believed the arrows originated. The White Rider hopped from the branch to grab on to a vine and slid down towards the ground. Another arrow was fired that severed the vine in two. Archeus found himself falling again but recovered much better this time by grabbing onto a second vine. Archeus sprinted across the dense path as he dodged arrows. An explosive arrow zipped passed him and detonated on a tree causing it to fall in Archeus' path. He slid to a stop and turned around to fire an arrow himself. The arrow had a fire enchantment placed upon it that ignited a line of fire. The line separated himself from his attackers and gave him a chance to pick his targets. One of the archers was de-cloaked as they jumped across the line of mystic fire. The Horseman kicked the humanoid reptile in his chest sending him to the ground.

They were like the ones early but more . . . advanced. Their skin was still made up of scales but their faces were flatter and had more humanoid features then the ones before. It seems like these reptile archers were apart of some new generation. Archeus placed **Nemesis** on his back and pulled out his short swords for the close-quarters-combat. The archers pulled out their daggers for combat. Sparks flew from the blades making contact. Archeus parried an attack and sliced the arm off of one reptile as he took on more. They continued to jump through the fire in an attempt to overwhelm the rider. They must not know that he is one of the Four, they're use to taking on hundreds of adversaries at one time. So a few dozen is nothing to them. It seemed like this was about to be a dragged out slug-fest until a voice cried out. "Enough!!!" All the archers stayed their hands and stood down. Archeus removed his blades from the reptiles' throats and placed his short swords in their sheaths. The ring of fire dissipated as the leader of the misfits crossed over to reveal himself. "I'm Naxus, leader of these guerrilla fighters." "I'm Archeus rider of the . . ." Naxus cut him off, "I know who you are and I don't care. What are you doing in my realm?" "I was sent here on orders to destroy a portal, a portal that leads to Earth," said Archeus. Naxus lowered his scaly head in thought for a moment. "You know what I'm talking about don't you?" Naxus nodded, "I do and I know where it is." Archeus' expression brightened, "where is it." Naxus pondered for another moment, "it lies within the Jungle's Mouth but there is a problem. They've captured my brother and I fear that if we attack they will kill him."

The archers still had their arrows trained on the Horseman as he conversed with their master. "What does it matter to me what happens to your brother I could care less," Archeus responded harshly. "You should be concerned because I know the way to the Jungle's Mouth and you don't, Archeus. You need me and I need you." The White Rider didn't want his help but he did need it. Besides, a snake is a snake whether it slithers on its stomach or walks on two feet. He was out of choices and this was the only way to find the portal. "I will help you, Naxus. But as soon as you double-cross me I will kill you." Naxus grinned, "who said anything about a double-cross." Archeus took the grin as a for sure sign that it was coming. "Right this way my friend," Naxus said. The White Rider and the pack of reptilian archers moved through the trees like it was second nature. They swung from branch to another and bounced to others. Some could reach another branch that could be twenty to thirty feet away. Archeus watched his movements until he did it himself. But he could go even further because of his natural abilities. The Horseman bounded over the entire pack and landed in front of them all. The lizards leapt pass the rider as they continued on their journey.

Naxus held a fist up to signal his men to stop. They all stopped on command and waited for further orders. Naxus gestured for Archeus to follow as they moved further ahead of the pack. They stopped just before the cliff that lead into the valley below and into the Jungle's Mouth. Strange winged creatures flew around as other exotic creatures roared. "There," he pointed. Archeus peered in the direction and spotted the place they were looking for. He could feel the pure mystical energy that poured from the portal. "If that's the place then where are the ones holding your brother captive?" Archeus wondered.

"The ones who guard the portal are known as the Guardians. They are masters of stealth and can be hiding anywhere. These killers are armed with blowpipes and the darts are poisoned especially for lizards." Archeus looked at Naxus and knew why he didn't assault the Jungle's Mouth before. Naxus put a hand to his head and winced in pain. "What is it?" Archeus asked Naxus. "My brother he's in danger we must act now!" The guerrilla leader ordered his men into the valley below. "With such urgency Naxus must have a brother," Archeus thought. The guerrilla pack descended into the valley below and camped out in the trees to scout the area. The valley was silent except for the noise of the ambient jungle all around them. Archeus aimed a magic arrow into the air and fired. In mid-flight the arrow exploded sprinkling a red dust all over the area around the Jungle's Mouth. "The dust will cover anything that is a threat to us," the rider explained. The dust did as the Horseman said. The Guardians glowed bright enough for them to see in the jungle sun. They were surprisingly humanoid except for their unusually large size, claw-like feet and hands. "Pick your targets well," Naxus ordered. The guerrilla archers aimed for the guardians and prepared to fire. Archeus aimed *Nemesis*, "That's the same for you too." Naxus dropped his hand and the arrows flew into the Jungle's Mouth. Cries of pain resonated in the humid sky. A dart slammed into the neck of an archer killing him instantly. Arrows and darts streaked through the trees. The shadow arrows that Archeus shot could course-correct themselves mid-flight going around things in the way. Archeus never missed a shot with his bow. More and more bodies fell to the grass as the fighting continued.

The Guardians were no fools they zipped back and forth from their positions after each shot they took. "We need to move out of these trees there's not enough cover," Archeus said dodging darts. "I know that!" Naxus yelled. The guerrilla leader ordered his men down to ground level and they formed a wide crest around the Jungle's Mouth. The archers took cover behind rocks as they continued to shoot at the Guardians. Archeus was still in the trees as he watched the battlefield. That's when he noticed the Guardians flanking the guerrilla fighters on their right. The Horseman moved fast through the trees leaping from the branch to a vine and swung to the ground. His bow was placed on his back and his short swords were drawn. He sliced through their flesh like butter and brought more to their knees. The White Rider zoned out as his eyes were combat glazed, racking up more kills. He jammed the blade into a Guardian's leg and threw him into another one. Archeus sensed the other Guardians approaching the left flank. His short sword started vibrating before he launched it into the air. The short sword arched mid-flight to dodge the guerrilla archers and shortly after struck the Guardians. The weapon slapped back into his hand and they were placed back into their sheaths. The bewildered reptilians looked at the Horseman wondering how he did that. Archeus simply looked at them with an expression that said 'huh?' As Archeus stepped closer and closer to the cave entrance he could feel the portal's energy grow. He crossed through the mouth of the cave to see the portal standing at the very back. A sharp numbing pain surged through his back before the Horseman doubled over. "We needed you to help us get to the portal and gain control over it. We're tired of this world we want a new one. And you helped us retrieve exactly what we needed but now you're no longer useful to me," Naxus said. The guerrilla leader ordered some of his men over to take out his trash. They knocked Archeus unconscious and picked up his body. "Take care of him," Naxus ordered. "How sir?" the archer asked. "Feed him to our pet." The archers nodded and dragged Horseman's body into the jungle. They dragged the rider far out into the jungle. They stopped at a pit where a very vicious beast waited for lunch. The reptilian archers slapped the rider over his head until he woke up.

Archeus woke up to the sight of the ugly creatures standing over him. "At the bottom of that pit awaits your end," the lizard said. The Horseman smirked, "And that dart holds your end." The reptile looked up to see a dart slam into his forehead. Another dart hit the other archer in his back. Both reptiles were dead and the rider was safe for now. Archeus stood to his feet as his liberators descend from their vantage points above. There was one that wore a mask of gold and commanded the rest. He stood directly in front of Archeus and addressed him. "I am Arczull, commander of the Guardians and soul protectors of the portal for centuries. Sadly, it took a single Horseman to rob us of that duty." "I have no excuse for what happened back there. All I ask for now is your help?" Archeus asked. Arczull contemplated for moment before coming to a conclusion. "Come Horseman we must move quickly." Archeus straightened his poster and shook Arczull's large hand. It was time for Archeus to undo all of his wrong that transpired that day. With his new found allies he would take back the portal and finish his mission.

The sun was high in the sky and beaming down on The Jungle's Mouth. Sentries stood in front of the cave entrance watching intensely. Their eyes were weary and they were glad that they were about to change shifts soon. A figure zipped in between the trees in the valley before them. One archer tapped his partner drawing their bows. "Alert the others," one said to the other. The archer raised his bow high preparing to fire. One dart killed an archer as the other one was able to fire his arrow before going down himself. The arrow soared high into the sky and exploded with a loud bang. Naxus knew what the bang meant and immediately issued orders to his men. Reptilian archers poured out of the cave entrance like vomit and formed a perimeter. "Steady, do not fire until you see those righteous defenders," Naxus commanded. They continued to watch as figures zipped back and forth within the tree line. The leaves stopped rustling causing silence for a moment. Out of the tree line came darts and arrows descending upon the lizards who were caught completely by surprise. Some archers were filled with darts while others were filled with arrows.

"Shoot! Shoot!" Naxus yelled. Arrows and darts flew back and forth across the valley towards intended targets. Archeus tapped Arczull on the shoulder, "Get ready to send your men." Arczull nodded as he signaled his men to get ready. Archeus at first fired an arrow that blinded the reptiles and then he fired three explosive arrows that impacted the enemy position. "Kill the lizards!!!" Arczull roared. The Guardians dropped down to the ground and advanced on the guerrilla archers. Guardians and Reptiles engaged in close-quarters-combat. Archeus swung into the battle below and pounced on Naxus. The reptile leader shoved the Horseman off scrambling to his feet. "I truly believed that you were killed Rider but I should've known better. Now I have to kill you myself." Naxus pulled out a sword that had a wicked blade meant for separating limb from body. Archeus drew his short swords, "You can't kill a Horseman child." The two of them rushed each other until their blades met. Sparks flew as swords clanged against one another in the area of war. Naxus deflected hit after hit as Archeus rained down the blows.

The guerrilla leader was exceptionally skilled with sword but Archeus was even more skilled. The White Rider increased the speed of his attacks to displace Naxus and take him out of rhythm. The two combatants met in a blade-lock that sent sparks flying. "You won't rob me of my future, my goals. I will enter the realm of Man and start a new kingdom!" Naxus spun around slamming his tail across Archeus' face sending him to the ground.

"Archeus!" Arczull shouted, "Naxus ran into the cave. Me and my men can handle this." Archeus nodded and ran into the cave after the reptile commander. He was met by five guerrilla archers but they were quickly taken care of. Out of nowhere a barrage of arrows zipped towards Archeus. The rider reacted quickly with a graceful spinning move that deflected all arrows and then kicked Naxus hard in his chest. He slammed into the stone wall of the cave, enraging him. The lizard threw his sword down and extended his claws which were more sinister then his sword. Naxus swiped repeatedly at the Horseman with extreme prejudice. "I am tired of you Archeus. You and your fellow riders think that you are the cosmic law but in truth you are all nothing but expendable grunts!" Archeus' short swords begun to glow with an ghostly white as his temper grew short. His combat glazed eyes started sparking with electricity as he went on the offensive. Archeus moved so fast that every single move blurred into another. The Horseman sliced through all of his claws and slammed the reptiles face into the stone ground. Naxus rolled over with blood seeping from his mouth, snout, ears, and eyes. "I'm not the law. I just enforce it," Archeus said firmly. The White Rider ended Naxus' life with one powerful stomp. The lizard commander was no more. Archeus fired a electric arrow into the portal destroying it. He placed **Nemesis** on his back. The Guardians had secured victory in the Jungle's Mouth ending the battle. "Thank you Horseman for all your help. Now please leave this realm," Arczull said with a grin. "You don't have to tell me twice Guardian. Take care of this place Arczull this is the only home you know," Archeus responded. The White Rider conjured a portal leading to his own home. The quest for the portals is finally done. The Horseman can finally rest now. Even if it is for a century or two.

www.ingramcontent.com/pod-product-compliance
Lightning Source LLC
Chambersburg PA
CBHW071329130626
46556CB00004B/1819